134
4736869
$1.95

Silhouette Desire

LINDA McKE

Wilderness Passion

0-671-47368-9

"One Man's Folly May Be Another's Blessing."

Libby's heart leaped wildly as he reached out, his thumb gently tracing the natural curve of her cheek, coming to rest beneath her chin. Pleasurable tingles leaped like electricity through her tense body at his knowing touch. He searched her face for a long moment, as if memorizing each detail and nuance of her features.

"You're so beautiful, Libby," he whispered. "So alive . . . so damned enticing and yet so dangerous . . ." His mouth descended, grazing her parting lips like a feather.

Her senses reeled at the touch of his mouth and she felt his hand steadying her, pulling her forward against his body . . .

LINDSAY McKENNA

enjoys the unusual, and has pursued such varied interests as fire fighting and raising purebred Arabian horses, as well as her writing. "I believe in living life to the fullest," she declares, "and I enjoy dangerous situations because I'm at my best during those times."

Dear Reader:

SILHOUETTE DESIRE is an exciting new line of contemporary romances from Silhouette Books. During the past year, many Silhouette readers have written in telling us what other types of stories they'd like to read from Silhouette, and we've kept these comments and suggestions in mind in developing SILHOUETTE DESIRE.

DESIREs feature all of the elements you like to see in a romance, plus a more sensual, provocative story. So if you want to experience all the excitement, passion and joy of falling in love, then SIL-HOUETTE DESIRE is for you.

Karen Solem
Editor-in-Chief
Silhouette Books

LINDSAY McKENNA
Wilderness Passion

Silhouette Desire
Published by Silhouette Books New York
America's Publisher of Contemporary Romance

Silhouette Books by Lindsay McKenna

Captive of Fate (SE #82)
Chase the Clouds (DES #75)
Love Me Before Dawn (IM #44)
Wilderness Passion (DES #134)

SILHOUETTE BOOKS, a Division of Simon & Schuster, Inc.
1230 Avenue of the Americas, New York, N.Y. 10020

Copyright © 1984 by Eileen Nauman

Distributed by Pocket Books

ISBN: 0-671-47368-9

First Silhouette Books printing May, 1984

10 9 8 7 6 5 4 3 2 1

America's Publisher of Contemporary Romance

Printed in the U.S.A.

1

Libby frowned, unconsciously pushing a golden strand of hair away from her cheek. She sat behind her large executive desk, glaring at four different piles of documents, all marked IMPACT STATEMENT. Forcefully exhaling in frustration, she got up, circled her plush office and glanced out the window. It was nearly four P.M. on Friday afternoon and she could hardly wait for the business week to end. On Wednesday her boss, Doug Adams, had informed her that he had another project requiring her immediate attention. Her brown eyes had darkened with worry at the news. How could she possibly handle a fifth assignment?

"Look at it this way, Libby dear," Doug had replied in his usual amiable tone, "Cascade Amalgamated is a very progressive corporation, and nowhere is it busier than in the forestry division. Besides, in the year you've been with us you've been indispensable, and we're proud of your work. The vice-president of the forestry division thought that the state land lease we just acquired ought to fit nicely into your field. Plus, you need some vacation, and you'll certainly get it with this project. Just look at the weeks you'll be spending up in that magnificent Idaho wilderness as a holiday." He had smiled brilliantly, given her a mock salute and left her standing dumbfounded.

Libby glanced guiltily at the stacks of documents that required her attention. One more project, she thought distractedly.

She chewed on her lower lip momentarily and then closed her eyes. Her lashes, the color of wheat in midsummer, lay like thick fans against her high cheekbones. She pirouetted on her long legs and walked back to the window, which overlooked San Francisco Bay. The evening fog was beginning to creep in from the ocean, making it look as if the sky were pulling a white wool blanket over the Pacific. It was August and the cloud cover would be welcome, taking the edge off the day's heat. Libby desperately wanted to have a weekend that wasn't spent doing office work. She touched the back of her chignon in a nervous gesture.

"Dr. Stapleton?"

Libby swung around, startled. "Yes, Betty?"

Her secretary gave a small apologetic smile, stepping inside the door momentarily. "Remember the man who was supposed to have kept the ten-o'clock appointment with you this morning? Mr. Dan Wagner?"

Libby rolled her eyes upward. "Don't tell me he's here *now.*"

Betty nodded. "I'm afraid he is. And, judging from his

angry looks, he's none too happy about it. Shall I send him in?"

Groaning inwardly, Libby smoothed the white lab coat she always wore over her business clothes. "Yes. Leave any phone messages for me on your desk. When I get out of here tonight, I'll check through them."

Her secretary, a woman close to her own age, added, "You'd think he would have the good manners to call back on Monday, not last thing Friday afternoon."

Libby tried to straighten up the obvious clutter on her desk. Why did each of the four piles of documents resemble miniature leaning Towers of Pisa? "I have to see him, Betty. He's the forestry manager for the latest lease we bought. Do me a favor and bring us both coffee, I'm afraid it's going to be a long meeting."

"Sure. Want me to order some sandwiches too?"

Libby managed a wry smile, her full lips curving upward. "I'm not intending to stay *that* long. Coffee will do fine."

He came through the door without making a sound. As lean as a mountain lion, he moved with boneless grace. Libby stood frozen behind her desk, fingertips resting on the smooth surface, staring up at him like a wide-eyed child. A pulse leaped at the base of her throat as she met his eyes. They were a deep, thundercloud blue, and his hair was dark and slightly curly, with red highlights. Perhaps what struck her the most were the rugged features of his face. That face belonged to a man who regularly challenged nature and won. Dark eyebrows and thick lashes partially hid the anger she knew he was controlling. His nose was straight except for a bump that indicated it had been broken once. Libby gave an inner sigh of relief when she saw that his well-shaped mouth was turned up at the corners and not downward. He must laugh once in a while, she thought. And small laugh lines around the corners of his eyes confirmed her guess. It gave her the necessary courage to walk around the desk, her hand extended in greeting.

"Mr. Wagner, I'm Dr. Elizabeth Stapleton. Please, come in and have a seat."

Her long fingers were cool in comparison to the warm, callused strength of his hand. Her voice, usually husky, sounded almost breathless now, and Libby reprimanded herself. But then, the man standing and studying her with catlike intensity would make anyone feel slightly nervous.

He released her fingers—almost reluctantly, she thought. "I didn't realize you would be a woman," he said, his tone hard and without compromise. "E. Stapleton. That's how the damn letter was signed." Dan controlled his sense of frustration. How was he supposed to harvest a forest with a woman who looked more like a lovely child than someone who knew the timber industry? Despite the coolness of his manner, something wrenched at his heart when he looked into her clear, almost unlined face. Reason dictated that she was older than she looked, and he smiled to himself. She was all business, but he sensed that she was nervous. One part of him felt badly about being hard on her. But another part of him, the forestry manager, was concerned only with efficiency. Up in those mountains, the only thing that mattered was action—quick, decisive action. And now he was saddled with a woman who had probably never stepped out of her office. Damn.

Libby girded herself against his attack. How many times had she heard that for openers? "Please sit down," she entreated, her brown eyes narrowing slightly in self-defense. "I'm sure you're tired from the trip."

Dan Wagner remained standing, one hand resting loosely on his hip. There was absolutely nothing conciliatory about him. He wore a set of tightly fitting blue jeans, which emphasized his long, muscular thighs, and a western plaid shirt with a corduroy blazer thrown over it, as if to appease society to a certain degree.

Libby was amazed at the breadth of his chest and the strength that was so evident in his proudly thrown-back shoulders. He looked like he could carry the weight of the world on them and never tire. He gave her a thin smile, his eyes glittering. "You're right about the trip, but I'm tired of sitting. And if I have my way about this meeting, I won't be here long enough to get the urge to sit down."

Leaning back in her black leather chair, she pointed toward the forms and files just given to her by Doug Adams. "This is going to take at least two hours," she warned, her voice hardening slightly to emphasize the point. "We have to discuss a myriad details on collecting data for the environmental-impact statement on State Land Lease Number 4293." She forced herself to smile. "So why don't you relax for a moment while I ask my secretary to get the maps we'll need?"

Libby gladly escaped the tense atmosphere of her office. The man was seething with barely restrained anger, and it was all focused on her. What had she done? It was Friday afternoon and all she wanted to do was go home and sleep for the next twenty-four hours. Peeking around the corner, she called, "Betty, get me those maps of the Sleeping Deer Mountain area, will you?"

He was pacing restlessly around her office when she returned, and her heart hammered as he lifted his chin, fixing her again with his impenetrable stare. "Was your flight late?" she inquired, thinking of the unkept appointment earlier that morning.

"No," came the cool reply, "I just had other, more important tasks that required my attention first." He shook his head. "I think this whole thing is a fiasco, Dr. Stapleton. Cascade Amalgamated has been given the rights to lease the land and harvest the timber. I'm too damn busy to come here and chitchat and then to baby-sit you or one of your city-bred assistants on a three-week interior study up on Sleeping Deer Mountain."

Libby wiped her sweaty palms on the sides of her white coat. Dan Wagner presented a combination of impatience and masculinity that sent her senses reeling with unexplained pleasure. He was quietly handsome in a rugged, outdoorsy fashion, something she had seen very rarely in the Bay area, where she'd lived all her life. She was used to men in Savile Row suits and silk ties who spoke with cultured brevity and diplomacy. It was obvious that none of that could be expected from the forestry manager. He was a man more comfortable with an ax in his hand than trading glib comments.

"Mr. Wagner, I'm afraid neither of us have any say on these impact studies. Officially we are teammates on the Deer Mountain project until its completion."

He shoved his hands in his jean pockets. "Look, Doctor, under any other circumstance I wouldn't mind meeting you." That was true. Rarely had he seen someone of such incredible beauty. Dan wondered how she could have majored in biology when she should have been a model for all the international fashion magazines. She certainly didn't belong in that office. And certainly not in his world.

Savagely Dan reminded himself that he was a simple country boy who had barely graduated from high school and then earned his forestry management through harsh experience. It was evident that Dr. Elizabeth Stapleton was not only beautiful but also intelligent. And that combination made him feel mildly threatened. "You can take that doctorate in biology, the EPA and those damn impact-study demands and shove them. I don't need my logging operation held up for a whole damn year because you have to count bugs, animals and plants and try to tell me how to do a job I've done for the last fifteen years."

Libby colored fiercely, her flawless Swedish complexion turning ruddy over his irate words. Clenching her fists at her sides, she tried to temper her retort. "Mr. Wagner, I don't care what you think about the study, but I do care when you insult me. I won't stand here and argue with you." She lifted her chin, her brown eyes dark with fury. "I have an idea," she whispered tautly. "It's been a long week for both of us, I'm sure. Why don't you come back here Monday morning after a good rest and we'll discuss this problem reasonably."

Dan Wagner tilted his head, as if viewing her in a new

light. His turbulent blue eyes lost their initial darkness and one corner of his mouth pulled upward. "So, you've got some backbone after all."

Libby compressed her lips. "Shall we get off the personal level, Mr. Wagner?" she demanded.

He smiled, but the warmth did not reach his eyes. "That's hard to do, Doctor, you're a good-looking woman. Biologist or not."

Her heart thudded at his backhanded compliment. At twenty-nine she was used to men complimenting her on her natural Scandinavian beauty. But for some reason Dan Wagner's sincerity shook her off center, and she lost some of her composure, blushing. Irritated, she turned, facing the window and crossing her arms against her chest. "I'll see you at eight A.M. sharp Monday morning, Mr. Wagner."

A few seconds passed and there was no answer. Libby unfolded her arms, making a half-turn toward him, confused by his sudden silence. Damn, he was irritating!

Wagner walked over to her desk, glancing at the other documents idly. He picked up one thick blue book, frowning. "Looks like they keep you pretty busy here," he commented.

"Too busy," she agreed evenly. "And to be honest, Mr. Wagner, I didn't want your project. I have enough to do."

He laid the book back down, his callused, work-worn hand resting against it. "Good. Then we both agree that this doesn't have to be done. Which means I don't have to stay and I don't have to come back here Monday morning."

Betty knocked timidly on the office door and entered when Libby called to her. Taking the maps, Libby cleared a space on her desk for the two rolls. "Mr. Wagner, you either talk to me now or later. This impact study has to be done." And then she met his glare fearlessly. "Or do you want to go before the board of inquiry and tell them why we didn't do the study as the state regulations require? I'm afraid we can no longer log these leases as we've done in the past. And what would you say to the president of our company when the state of Idaho leveled a couple of million dollars' worth of fines at us for not following guideline procedures? Not to mention the fact that they would surely sue Cascade Amalgamated without a blink of their eye. I guarantee it. That is the very least you can count on, Mr. Wagner."

Dan's mouth thinned in displeasure as he continued to hold her gaze. "You know your stuff, don't you, Doctor?" he ground out. "I could sidestep you and give my men the order to start logging, but then, when the state caught us, you'd sit at my trial, smiling like—"

Libby shook her head. "I would be there defending you! I'm a company biologist and you are under my jurisdiction. The state would hold the president of our company responsible. It's as simple as that."

Some of her initial fear of him was subsiding and she walked around the desk, leaning against it as she met his gaze. "You're forgetting the worst of it. Our lease would be forfeited and so would the money we've put down on that agreement." She shrugged her shoulders. "Cascade probably has somewhere close to thirty million tied up in that deal right now. We'd lose everything. Plus, we would never be able to bid on another state leasing program in Idaho, and that would put a real damper on the company's expansion program for our forestry division."

Dan walked over to her bookcase, glancing at the books in passing. He stopped at the window. "You know," he said, his voice less harsh, "I've logged all over this world and I've never run into the red tape that we have here in the States." He ran his strong, lean fingers through his hair. "Why can't they just let us go in and take the mature timber and get out?"

"Because," Libby said, sounding even to herself like a teacher, "those mountains will need reseeding to stop erosion. Once erosion starts, the whole ecological balance will be affected, from the bugs on down to the plants you mentioned earlier."

Dan gave her a brief, irritated glare. "You sound real good on tape, Doctor, but I wonder how long you'll last out there in those mountains."

Libby felt her stomach knot. She had never been in a situation that required her to backpack into an area to initiate a study. Her experience was with shopping centers, construction on buildings and airports. It was an eight-to-five job that she could leave at the end of the day. And when she left she went home to her Palo Alto apartment and slept in her own comfortable bed. She grimaced inwardly. This assignment meant hiking into the interior and camping out for three weeks.

"Mr. Wagner, I don't like this any more than you do." She sighed, straightening up. "Which will it be? Tonight or Monday?"

"Right now. This is the last time I ever want to have to

come to this damn place. Let's get down to the brass tacks of it, Doctor."

Glancing at her watch, Libby noted it was nearly nine o'clock. Darkness was finally stealing the last remnants of dusk away, leaving the scintillating lights of San Francisco sparkling like jewels along the bay. They had sat across from each other like adversaries. Each time she brought up another point of the impact study, he argued strongly against it until her cooler reasoning prevailed. He saw no point in testing vegetation stability, soil erodibility or soil chemistry. Pain throbbed across her forehead and she rubbed her brow slowly.

"Headache?" Dan inquired, most of the animosity out of his tone.

Libby relaxed against the back of her chair, managing a weary smile. "It's been one of those weeks," she admitted.

"And I'm sure I topped it off," he said, getting to his feet.

Libby watched him stretch like an awakening feline and walk lithely toward the door. He hadn't said it by way of apology, only as a flat statement of fact. More than one logger had had a few choice words to say about impact studies and biologists getting in the way of logging operations with their bureaucratic drivel. But none of them had regarded her the way he was doing as he turned and studied her in the gathering silence. Right now she felt like one of those bugs under a microscope.

"So when are you coming up to initiate the study, Doctor?" he asked, and then a cruel smile drifted across his features. "Or will it be one of your city-bred assistants?"

She managed a cutting smile. "No, I'll be coming."

He pursed his lips, leaning lazily against the door. "You look pretty athletic. Nice, strong legs. You're taller than the average woman, so you ought to have a decent stride on you. What do you weigh, around one hundred and thirty pounds, Doctor?"

Libby felt her face growing warm again and she shifted uncomfortably in the chair. Dan Wagner had a way of making her feel naked before his scrutinizing eyes. "Close to that," she murmured, confused by his cryptic question. "Why?"

Wagner threw her an acid smile of contempt. "You ever backpacked?"

"No."

"I could be a real bastard and make you find your own equipment, but I won't. I want to get in and get out of that study area just as fast as we can. I don't have time to play nursemaid to a tenderfoot. You're going to be excess baggage on this trip, and I might as well get you outfitted as best I can." He seemed to be thinking out loud more than talking directly to her. "What's your shoe size?"

"Eight-and-a-half B."

"Ever walk more than a mile anywhere?" he drawled.

A glint of fire flared briefly in her brown eyes. "On occasion," she replied, stung.

"Then you'd better start walking at least a mile every night and build up to the point where you can walk four miles in about an hour."

"This isn't some sort of marathon!" she shot back, sitting up in the chair.

Dan scowled. "Oh, yes it is, Dr. Stapleton. It's my race you're calling and I aim to have you in shape to take the punishment of a hundred-mile trek and still be able to take your damn samples of soil, water, insects and God knows what else."

Libby tried to ignore the sarcasm in his tone. She flipped open the pages of her calendar appointment book. "All right," she muttered, "name the day, Mr. Wagner."

Without batting an eye he replied, "Three weeks from now, Doctor. I'll pick you at the Challis, Idaho, airport at noon. Be there." He yanked open the door and then turned. "Oh, one more thing: Get some antivenom serum from your physician and bring it along with you. If you get bitten by a snake, I'll be damned if I'm going to haul your body out of the interior."

Libby opened her mouth and then snapped it shut, her brown eyes glittering with anger. He was so damn tough and uncompromising! She wearily touched her brow, reminding herself that one never got cooperation from others by lobbing insults back and forth. "I will do my level best not to become an albatross around your neck, Mr. Wagner."

Dan gave her a measuring look. "You hungry?"

The unexpected change in his tone and the question caught her off-guard. "Hungry?" she repeated stupidly. Why was she acting like an unsure teen-ager around this threatening male! It galled her. Perhaps it was the lateness of the hour, or her increased workload, or both. She wasn't sure.

His face lost some of its initial hardness as he studied her. "Yes, hungry." He consulted his watch. "It's after nine P.M. and I haven't eaten anything since noon." He slowly appraised her from head to toe, liking what he saw more than he should have. At that moment Dr. Elizabeth Stapleton looked vulnerable, and it moved him from his implacable stance. "My hotel is right around the corner, and they have a coffee shop that's open all night." He gave a slight shrug of his shoulders. "Besides, there's a list of things you should draw up that you'll need for this backpacking trip. I don't want you coming poorly equipped."

Libby detected the thaw in his voice and in his eyes. Her shoulders, drawn up from the tension, relaxed, and she forced a slight smile.

"All right, Mr. Wagner, I'll join you for a late dinner and we'll discuss the details of my trip to Challis." Her voice sounded wooden, even to herself, and she saw his eyes narrow. With a wave of her slender hand she murmured, "I'm sorry, it's just been one very long day. Let me get my purse and attaché case and then we can leave."

Libby bridled beneath his watchful stare as she went through the process of picking up the necessary items. She had never been made to feel so uncomfortable and yet thrilled by any man. And whether she wanted to admit it or not, she was glad of the invitation to dinner. It would give her a chance to try to establish a more congenial working relationship with this cougar of a forestry manager. She chose to ignore the second reason why she looked forward to the dinner: Dan Wagner was a breed of man she had never encountered, and she was fascinated by him. He reminded her of a thunderstorm: constantly changing and master of everything that he touched. A slight smile pulled at her lips as she switched off the office lights.

"I hope you're a little quicker about gathering articles in the field, Doctor."

Libby's heart sank, her head snapping up, meeting those glacier-blue eyes once again. Why was he continuing to snipe at her as if she were his enemy? She had an option: meet him head on in a clash of words or call a truce. The truce was infinitely more appealing.

"All right, Mr. Wagner, since you insist upon being frank and to the point, I'm going to be also." She walked to within a foot of where he stood out in the dimly lit hall. His face was shadowed. A sense of danger coupled with excitement washed over Libby. "I'm very tired tonight. And although your observations are well intended, I'm just not up to coping with your brutal assessments."

Dan studied her in the half-light, his eyes glittering with newfound interest. "Honesty," he murmured. "That's a rarity at the corporate-management level." He tilted his head. "Tell me, Doctor, how do you manage the politics around here if you're this honest all the time?"

Libby heard the genuine surprise in his voice, and she saw it reflected in his eyes for just a second. Either Wagner was paranoid or he had gotten shafted and shuffled around too many times by corporate people. He was a blunt man, but not as cruel as she had first thought. It was his way of getting to the heart of a problem. "I don't play politics very well, Mr. Wagner."

"That's obvious."

Libby met and matched his stare. She had to suppress a growing smile. "Thank you for the compliment. Now, do we have a deal? Will you keep your observations for another time when I'm better prepared to handle them in a positive way?"

Dan smiled. He slid his large, callused hand beneath her elbow, guiding her down the hall. "It's a deal, Doctor."

Dan had to remind himself to stop staring at her. Beneath the overhead fixtures of the stylish coffee shop, her golden hair blazed in a halo of light. The skin was drawn tightly across her cheekbones, showing her fatigue. Again he felt a prick of guilt over his abruptness with her. But dammit, Cascade Amalgamated had put him in an impossible position. His anger was aimed at her because she would be the millstone that he would have to wear during that journey into the interior. Still . . . Dan savagely quelled feelings that had been aroused simply by her quiet presence. He wrestled with those emotions, not having felt them in almost fifteen years. Grimly tightening his lips, he forced himself to tear his gaze from her and study the menu.

After ordering their meals, Dan rested his elbows on the table, meeting her gaze. "You ever been out in the forest?"

Libby shook her head. "If you call Golden Gate Park a forest, then I can qualify. Otherwise I'm afraid not."

He liked her sense of humor. It became her. What the hell was he doing keeping a list of what he did and did not like about her? Frustrated with himself, Dan continued to assess just how much of a problem she was going to be to him out in the forest.

"You're a biologist. I thought all of your kind hung out in the lonely, isolated edges of civilization."

"I'm a city biologist. All of my environmental-impact studies have been on suburban and city sites." Libby knew she should have kept that information to herself because his face tightened.

"The bug men I know prefer isolation to the city," he growled.

She smiled at his reference to biologists as "bug men." It was true: Many biologists spent untold hours out in the wilderness, setting up highly detailed studies to seek out nature's balance in a given area. "City-born and city-bred, I'm afraid, Mr. Wagner."

He gave a doleful shake of his head. "Then it makes you even more of a liability on this trip than I first thought. How in the hell do you expect to know what to look for out in the forest if you have no previous experience in that field, Doctor?"

Libby put a tight rein on her temper. "That's a fair question," she said. She rested her chin on folded hands in front of her, holding his burning blue gaze. "I'm coming in to set up the management guidelines for the environmental-impact project. My job isn't actually to go out and do the studies; we'll get bids from firms who hire themselves out for that purpose. So, you see, my lack of experience isn't really a consideration in this case."

She was smart, Dan grudgingly decided. And she was unlike any woman he had ever met. "If you think on your feet this well, there may be some hope for you after all."

Libby smiled tiredly. "What are some of the items you wanted to discuss with me?" The waitress brought their orders, and between bites Libby made a list of what she needed. Later, over coffee, she pondered her growing list.

"So, what is the most important item here?"

"Boots," Dan answered emphatically. "Matter of fact, when you finish your coffee, I'm going to measure your feet. I'll get you the boots. I can't risk a tenderfoot buying the wrong pair and ending up with blisters the first day of hiking."

She raised one eyebrow in question. "Measure my feet?"

He barely nodded his head. "Yes. I have a tape measure up in my room. In Challis there's a good boot store. I'll take the information back and then send you a pair."

Libby hid a smile. Despite his gruffness, he seemed to be concerned—even if it was in his own defense. "I never realized that a boot could be that important."

"When you're carrying thirty to fifty pounds of gear on your back, Doctor, those boots had better feel just right to you. Otherwise you're either going to blister or bruise your feet." He pulled out some money to pay for the meal and then rose. "And like I said before, I'm not going to carry you *into* or *out of* the interior."

Libby rose, her heartbeat quickening. She wanted to say, "Just being around you is an adventure." It struck her as amusing that he was inviting her up to his room just to get fitted for a pair of hiking boots. She felt his hand on her elbow, gently guiding her out of the restaurant and into the plush lobby toward the bank of elevators. His body brushed against hers and she experienced a thrill of pleasure.

The hotel room was lit by one small lamp on a coffee table. Dan reached over, flipping on the main switch.

"Have a seat, Doctor. I'll be back in a moment."

Libby sat down on the small couch, her purse resting in her lap. She watched with interest as he brought an oversize notebook, a pencil and a small cloth tape measure. As he knelt at her feet he met her interested gaze.

"First things first." He reached over on the dresser and picked up two large pairs of gray socks. "Put these on," he ordered.

Libby leaned over, gently removing her high heels. Heat flowed from her neck up into her face as Wagner came within inches of her. She tried to disregard the hungry look that glittered in the depths of his eyes as he watched her struggle with the heavy socks.

"Why socks?" she protested.

"You always wear two pairs with any boot to protect your skin," he answered patiently. She had damn nice legs, he decided. But then, he had known that from the moment he had met her. There was something childlike in her struggles with the socks that brought a wry smile to his face.

Libby sat back. "There," she sighed. Her laughter was infectious as she looked down at them. "I must say, this doesn't look like the height of fashion."

Dan found himself returning her laughter. How could this woman who exhibited the elegance of San Francisco society suddenly lapse into self-deprecating humor? He liked people who could poke fun at themselves. He placed the notebook beneath her right foot, carefully drawing the outline of it.

"You like to laugh, don't you?"

Libby gave him a startled look. "Why—yes. Doesn't everyone?"

"No." He raised his head, drinking in her puzzled features. "Especially very beautiful, well-bred women who were raised with all the finer things of life."

Her honey-brown eyes took on a look of deviltry. "Just because you see me as a cosmopolitan snob, that doesn't mean I can't laugh or enjoy life, Mr. Wagner."

Dan grinned, maintaining a grip on her foot. He rested it on his long, well-muscled thigh. There was something primitive and stirring about touching her. He slid his hand down over her shapely calf. "Maybe there's hope for you after all, Doctor," he said blandly. "You know, you aren't in as bad shape as I thought," he said, more to himself than for her benefit, running his hand more firmly across her calf.

Libby blushed and compressed her lips. His touch acted like a hot brand on her nylon-clad skin. She could feel the rough texture of his fingers as they slid over her ankle. She wanted to pull away. She wanted him to continue. A tumult of emotion momentarily silenced her, and all she could do was stare at him.

Dan forced himself back to the business at hand. Taking the tape, he measured her slender ankle, the ball of her foot and the instep. Carefully marking down the information, he released her right foot. "What do you do, work out at a health spa?" he asked, reaching for her left foot and placing it on his thigh.

Libby swallowed, her heart pounding at the base of her throat. His touch was electric, triggering a myriad shocking and pleasant sensations within her body. "I—uh, yes, I work out three days a week."

He regarded her for a moment. "A city snob working

up a bit of a sweat? Doesn't that go against your image, Doctor?"

There was a pleasant tension building between them, and Libby could sense the fragile bond of trust. Since he approved so highly of honesty, she felt it best to remain on that tack. "You must hate city women."

Dan drew her foot on the paper. "Now, whatever gave you that idea?" he drawled.

"Your whole attitude, Mr. Wagner. Taking sniping shots at me because I do try to stay fit even though I sit at a desk all day long isn't necessary."

"It was a backhanded compliment. Most of the women I know are country-born and -bred. They're used to working. They have calluses on their hands."

Libby had the sudden urge to hide her hands so that he couldn't see her palms. She didn't have one single callus. "And city women are weak, lazy and snobbish in your book?"

He raised his head, his blue eyes darkening. "That was my general assessment until just now. You obviously aren't a weak woman, Doctor."

"Weak? In what sense of the word?" Why was she interested in what he thought of her?

"There aren't many women who care to stand up to me. Or men, for that matter."

She smiled wryly. "I can see why. The kitchen gets pretty hot where you're concerned."

Dan shrugged. "You even have some old-fashioned logic. I'm impressed, Doctor."

He finished measuring her left foot, his hand remaining around her ankle.

Libby pressed forward with her desire to know something of how Dan Wagner operated. She was acutely aware that her foot was resting on his thigh, his hand nonchalantly curled around her ankle. "So, you see me as a feminist?" she probed.

Reluctantly, Dan released her foot. "I have no qualms with a woman doing any job—provided she can do it."

"Then strong women don't get under your skin?"

A sliver of a smile touched his eyes as he watched her struggle out of the socks. "Contrary to popular opinion, Doctor, I like a woman who can stand on her own two feet."

Libby handed him the socks, her fingers brushing his momentarily. She felt the room getting warm. Or was it her? There was a dangerous tension lingering between them, and she was feeling flustered, unable to think as quickly as she might ordinarily. "You said you feel that city women are weak, lazy and snobbish. I just wanted to know how many of those adjectives apply to me, Mr. Wagner." She picked up her shoes, slipping them back on her nylon-clad feet.

"Well, if you're lazy, it will show up soon enough. Being out on the trail isn't for anyone who doesn't have stamina." He gave her a dark look. "And if you do manage to come through this experience in one piece, you'll earn my respect."

She rested both hands on her thighs, her eyes sparkling with challenge. "Obviously you don't see me finishing."

Wagner rose, standing over her. "Let's just say I'll

suspend my judgment of you, Dr. Stapleton. You've already shown you have a backbone."

He walked over to the door. "Come on, I'll walk you to your car."

Libby picked up her purse. "You don't have to." She gave him a slight smile. "We strong women can take care of ourselves."

Before she knew what had happened, she felt Dan Wagner's fingers on her shoulder. In one deft, seemingly lazy move he had imprisoned her within his strong, work-hardened hands. She was wildly aware of his fingers caressing the fabric at her shoulders. Her heart soared, her breathing suddenly uneven at his masculine closeness. Her eyes lifted upward to meet his dark, appraising stare.

"You know," he began softly, "you aren't strong in some ways, Doctor. I'll know by the time our hike is over just who and what you are and are not." The disturbing quality of his voice sent a dangerous thrill through her. She felt trapped, excited and frightened, all at the same time. Her body wouldn't react to her commands. She should move away . . . away from his dizzyingly male essence, which acted like an aphrodisiac to her awakening senses.

"Now," he continued amiably, "I'm going to walk you to your car. No protests, Doctor." He released her shoulder, his other hand on her elbow as he led her out the door.

Libby was at a loss for words. There was a commanding presence about Dan Wagner that simply defied description. She stole a look up at him once as they were walking down the street. In some ways he reminded her of a knight from the days of chivalry. In other ways he was a cougar on the prowl, and she felt as if she were his intended prey. . . .

On Tuesday morning Libby found a priority-mail package on her desk when she came to the office. Puzzled, she slipped the white smock on over her Qiana dress of pale pink. Betty bobbed inside the door. "Dr. Stapleton! That box just arrived. I wonder what's in it." She smiled brightly and stood at Libby's desk, waiting.

Libby returned the smile. There was no return address, simply her name scrawled almost illegibly across the brown paper in which the box was tightly wrapped. "I don't know." And then she laughed. "The postmark is from Challis, Idaho. . . ."

"Oh, from that gorgeous Dan Wagner, maybe? Oh, hurry, open it! I can't believe it: he sent you a gift. Isn't that wonderful?"

Knowing that Betty was about to be sadly disillusioned, Libby tore the paper wrapping off the huge box. A neatly folded note rested on top of the tissue paper. Peeking under the paper, Libby saw a pair of highly unflattering hiking boots in the box.

Betty's animated expression faded. "Boots?" she asked. "Is this his way of paying homage to you?" she giggled.

Returning the smile, Libby opened the note. "I doubt it. We got along like dogs and cats on Friday night," she confided to her secretary. "And he made it very clear that he wasn't going to coddle me during the time we'll have to spend together. These boots are his way of making sure I don't hold him back when we're hiking." A smile tugged at her lips as she met her secretary's bewildered gaze. "Where I'm going in three weeks, I'll be needing these."

Betty sniffed at the gift. "What a shame. He was so dashing and masculine. I guess his sort doesn't think to send a woman flowers. . . ."

Finally alone, Libby sat down, unfolding the note. Her fingers tingled as she opened the crisp white paper. Suddenly, she was anxious to read his letter.

"Dear Dr. Stapleton," it said:

These boots won't do your beauty justice, but they are practical. Wear them each day when you go for your walk. Remember, be sure to put on a pair of heavy wool socks so that you don't end up with blisters.

D.W.

A part of her felt rebuffed and hurt; another part of her laughed. Well, there was one thing that could be said about him: He was consistent. Infinitely practical, attentive to detail and as caustic as acid, Dan Wagner was certainly going to earn a corner of her memory. He reminded her of a rogue stallion that was used to having his way about everything. And then he had to run into her, a woman. It seemed obvious that he was used to dealing with women on only one level: the bed. He didn't enjoy dealing with her in his business world. She gently laid the note back on top of the boots, smiling to herself.

"Well, Dan, for better or worse, you're going to be saddled with me," she murmured. A glint of mirth danced in her brown eyes. "Serves you right."

Doug Adams rested his thin leg casually over the corner of Libby's desk, an amused smile on his long face. "Well, you about ready to graduate to the forestry level?" he asked her.

Libby pursed her lips and mentally went over the last-minute chores she had to attend to before she caught her plane at San Francisco International. "I hope so, Doug. I can't quite envision myself being in the woods for that long." Worriedly she lifted her gaze to meet his green eyes. "I feel terrible about leaving the office. Are you sure that Cherie can handle the necessary follow-up on my other four cases for that long? I mean, she's only just recently been made assistant. Isn't that quite a bit of pressure to put on someone?"

Doug shook his head. "Do you ever stop worrying? Relax, Libby. Frankly, if I were you, I'd be more anxious about having to work with Wagner." He watched her for a moment. "Have you heard from him?"

A grin touched her lips. "We've been trading cryptic notes for the past three weeks in preparation for this outing. Mr. Wagner doesn't believe in company biologists, impact studies or the EPA." She gave a laugh, shrugging her shoulders. "So you see, it will be a piece of cake."

Doug got up. "Don't let him buffalo you, Libby. Just stand your ground with the man. He's a hell of a manager and probably one of the best forestry experts in the Northern Hemisphere. But make him meet you on your turf."

Her brown eyes sparkled. "That's like getting a wild stallion to stand still while you saddle him. I'm sure I'll take my share of lumps from him, Doug. If I come back black and blue, just put a sympathy card on the desk for me."

2

⦁⦁⦁⦁⦁⦁⦁⦁⦁⦁⦁

Her excitement spiraled upward as the small Cessna Skyhawk circled the narrow airstrip on the outskirts of Challis. Libby felt adrenaline making her heart beat faster. The long flight from Boise to Challis had been beautiful; the mountains were clothed in dark-green capes of pine and evergreen. The various shades of green were breathtaking at five thousand feet as the plane slid around the higher peaks of the Salmon River mountain range. More than once her mind had turned toward the coming meeting with Dan Wagner. Would he be just as caustic as he had been in San Francisco? She grinned carelessly, almost anxious to do battle with him once again. After the four short notes they had exchanged with each other over business matters, Libby thought she detected a dry sense of humor in the man. She looked forward to observing him again.

The noon sunlight was blinding as she stepped from the Cessna onto the worn Tarmac surface of the landing apron. The wind was fresh, coming from a westerly direction, ruffling her hair, which had been tamed into a ponytail. Libby tried not to appear too anxious and helped the co-pilot dislodge her assorted suitcases from the luggage compartment.

She was about to lift the heaviest piece when an arm covered with dark hair appeared from the left. "Here," came a growl that could only belong to Dan Wagner, "let me get that for you." His callused fingers wrapped strongly about the handle, and Libby moved aside, startled.

She took a step back and was struck by the boyish look about him. His hair, tousled by the wind, glinted with gold and red highlights. The shirt he wore was blue and white checked, the neck open, displaying the dark hair at his throat. The sleeves were rolled high and she saw the flexing of his hardened muscles. There wasn't an ounce of fat on him, and his maleness was intoxicating to her suddenly confused senses. He cocked his head, studying her in the intervening silence.

"What's this? The good doctor speechless? Don't tell me the crisp mountain air has got your tongue? Or do you stare like that all the time?" A slight grin curled one corner of his mouth as he stood, enjoying her presence. He wanted to tell her that without the silly-looking white smock she wore at the office, she looked beautiful. He had been right: She did have a strong, athletic body, yet without a heavy bone structure. Her breasts were nicely shaped and in balance with her slender figure and tiny waist.

Libby took a swallow, having the good grace to blush over her poor manners. He was incredibly handsome. He had seemed out of place in the office and equally uncomfortable in city clothes. But now, standing against the backdrop of the wilderness and the mountains, he looked like the lord of it all. She managed a weak smile, avoiding his amused stare.

"Actually, I think it's the altitude," she lied. "I was just thinking how much a part of the environment you looked."

He picked up her other bag. "I suppose I can construe that as a compliment or an insult," he drawled.

Libby slid the strap of her third bag over her shoulder, trying to match his stride as he headed toward a battered, dust-covered Jeep in the parking lot. "It was a compliment," she said, breathlessly coming to a halt at the vehicle.

Dan glanced at her darkly, shoving the luggage into the back. "Hop in and hold on. You're in for a bruising ride."

Libby curbed her initial disappointment. No, he hadn't changed an iota. But in his notes to her, there had been a slight yielding, a hint that they might find some neutral territory between them.

"Strap in," he advised.

"Why?" she challenged.

Dan's glance slid to her as he backed out of the lot, heading the noisy Jeep in a northerly direction. "Your ignorance is already showing, Doctor."

Her eyes narrowed. "I don't like being called stupid, Mr. Wagner, not by you or anyone."

"I didn't say you were stupid. I said your ignorance

was showing. There's a big difference," he corrected. "It's nice to see that Ph.D.'s don't know everything."

She clenched her teeth, fighting down the fury that threatened to overcome her judgment. Good Lord, they were already fighting, and she hadn't been there for more than fifteen minutes! Calming herself, Libby murmured, "You're right, there is. Since you seem so enlightened about seat belt policy in Idaho, why don't you tell me?"

He pointed toward the approaching range of mountains towering to the left of them. Libby could see a single thin ribbon of dusty road winding here and there up into the high reaches of timber until it ultimately disappeared around the other side of the ridge. "See that?" he demanded.

"The road? Yes."

"That's where we have to go. It's rutted, potholed and incredibly dangerous because the timber trucks have used it too long and it's never been repaired. More than one truck or Jeep has been flipped over." He looked at her squarely for a moment.

Libby stared at him. "D-does it happen often?"

He offered her a cutting smile. "Best business for the local undertaker is loggers on choke chains who didn't watch their step, and stupid tourists who race up these timber roads. Enough said?"

"Enough said," she agreed mutely, effectively silenced.

Libby pressed herself into the seat, one hand wrapped tightly around the reinforcement bar on the side of the door and the other hand on the dash. She had expected him to drive up that tortuous road like a wild backwoods maniac, but he didn't. He negotiated the deep ruts with an ease she openly admired. At times she was mesmerized by the play of muscles in his forearms as he coaxed the Jeep through the Gordian knot of curves, ruts and steep inclines. His features were closed and unreadable, but she thought she detected a fierce glimmer of challenge in his restless blue gaze as he missed nothing surrounding them. A new feeling developed within her toward Dan Wagner: She would be safe with him in this frightening environment that would be her home for the next three weeks. Maybe her foray into the wooded interior wouldn't be so bad, because Dan would be there to protect her.

"Been using those boots I sent you?" he asked, breaking into her thoughts.

"What? Oh, the boots. Yes." She smiled, meeting his glance. "You never did send the bill for them. Let me know how much they were and I'll write you a check." A golden glint of humor danced in her brown eyes. "That is, if you trust me to write you a check that won't bounce."

Dan Wagner's features remained inscrutable. But for just a brief second Libby saw him thaw, and it left her breathless. Was he human after all?

"I don't send a woman a gift and expect her to pay for it."

Libby's eyes widened. "B-but—" she stammered, not wanting to owe him anything, "I did some shopping at a few backpacking outlets in San Francisco, and a good pair costs upwards of—"

"What's the matter, Doctor, do you think the gift means you owe me something in return?" he asked.

Stung, Libby gasped. "I—"

"I know, you're one of those liberated women who can make their own way in the world. They don't like to owe anything to anyone. Especially a chauvinistic man like myself." He caught her startled gaze. "Correct, Doctor?"

His insight was like a knife being thrust into her heart and then twisted. Libby lowered her eyes, momentarily stunned and hurt by his cruelty. He must hate her badly. That discovery shook her to the core. She had made many friends during her life and prided herself on her ability to get along with everyone. Friend or foe. But this man was not even going to give her a chance. She had few defenses to protect herself from someone like him. City life had not prepared her to compete in the harsh environment of the forest. His forest, she corrected herself. Desperately she tried to come up with a way of dealing with his caustic personality. If she played the meek female, he would run all over her. The work that had to be done would never be accomplished. On the other hand, if she brazenly challenged him in his own domain, he would win. She wouldn't make it through the woods without his cooperation.

Libby shifted unconsciously in the bucket seat, searching for other possible approaches. She had to learn something more about Dan Wagner in order to understand why he operated the way he did. That would take some careful probing on her part. Perhaps then she could overcome enough of his animosity toward her to get her job done.

She decided to ignore his jibe and took a deep breath, initiating a new conversation as they pulled over the last hill on the ridgeline. "Have you always lived near a forest?"

Dan shifted the Jeep into low gear as they began a steep descent on the other side of the range. "I was born near here."

"Oh? Where exactly?"

"Salmon, Idaho. It's a small town northeast of Challis."

"I see. So you've lived in the mountains all your life?"

"Practically."

Libby caught her lower lip between her teeth. So far, so good, she told herself, realizing that the palms of her hands were wet with perspiration. "Have you always wanted to be a forester?"

Dan gave her a suspicious sidelong glance. "It was drilled into me a long time ago to stick to my own kind and stay on the side of the tracks I was born on. I've always lived in the country and the forests were always nearby. Why?"

"Just curious," Libby answered quickly. Too quickly. Wagner's blue eyes darkened considerably as he took stock of her.

"Are we playing twenty questions, Doctor? When you get done with yours, do I get to ask mine?"

Libby brightened at the thought. At least he was willing to play along. "Why not? I'm game."

An unwilling smile tugged at the corner of his mouth. "I'll give you that," he muttered. "All right, so far you've asked me three questions, Doctor. It's my turn to ask you three. Right?"

Libby gave a brief nod of her head, suddenly feeling uncomfortable. "Of course."

He shifted down again and the Jeep bucked to a near halt as they crawled around a particularly deep hole in the road. Now Libby began to appreciate his advice. If a tourist had come over that rise at forty miles an hour and hit the hole, he would have easily broken an axle and flipped his vehicle.

"Is there a man in your life?" Dan asked.

Libby's honey-brown eyes widened for a second while she digested the question. "Well . . ."

"Be fair about this. I answered yours without hesitation," he prodded.

Blushing, Libby said, "I had the respect to ask you questions that were less personal in nature, Mr. Wagner."

He smiled the smile of a wolf. "You didn't lay down any rules when we decided to play this game. Correct?"

"Yes," she grated.

"Then answer my question."

She wanted to hurl back "Why should you care?" but didn't. Instead she simply said, "No."

He seemed pleased with himself. Go ahead, Libby thought, sit there looking like the cat who ate the canary. So help me, I'm going to stuff it back down your throat someday soon. . . . Realizing where her attitude was taking her, she grew horrified. This was no way to conduct a business venture! She had worked before on projects in which she had to get along with men who didn't particularly care for her being a woman in a man's world. Admittedly there weren't many times when that had occurred, and certainly no man had blatantly attacked her like Wagner.

"Okay, second question: Are you divorced? Do you have children?"

"That's two!" she flared, incensed at his audacity.

"That will amount to my three questions, then, Doctor."

Libby wanted to curse. Her jaw hardened as she considered the ramifications of answering his intimate questions about her private life. If she didn't, she would lose the chance to find out what made him operate the way he did. Sighing in resignation, she responded.

"Yes, I am divorced, and no, I don't have any children. Satisfied?"

Dan gave her a lazy smile. "Care to elaborate?"

"That's four. I don't owe you another one!" she shot back.

The smile reached his eyes. "What's the matter, Doctor, is the game getting too serious for you? Or did you figure that a logger having nothing more than a high school diploma wouldn't understand your games? Never mind, you don't have to answer that one. I think I've made my point."

Libby gave him a brittle, fixed smile. Tears pricked at the back of her eyes. "The point, Mr. Wagner, is that you hate me and my kind. You've brought that home very succinctly. And no, I don't want to play our little game any more, because you have no concept of what fair play is all about. It has nothing to do with the degree of education at all. I never implied that loggers were stupid." Her voice shook with anger. Or was it suppressed tears?

Dan frowned, feeling guilty about his tactics. He saw the hurt clearly written on her face and wanted to apologize. Damn, what was he doing? She was simply trying to create a more friendly atmosphere between them. Why was he so ready to be defensive? Libby

Stapleton had done nothing to deserve his acid comments. Maybe he was threatened by her credentials and intelligence. In his experience beautiful faces meant no brains. But that wasn't the case this time. Cursing himself, Dan wanted to reach out and touch Libby's arm in apology. He wasn't much on words. But he knew he could convey his feeling through touch. Glancing over at her, Dan felt his body tighten with desire and he hesitated. Libby reminded him of a child in many ways, but she also had the inbred strength of a one-of-a-kind woman, and that attracted him tremendously.

He drove the Jeep off the last foothill and they entered a small grassy valley. It was warmer there, and the sun-dappled meadow waved with patches of blue lupine, foxglove and larkspur. Desperately Libby concentrated on keeping back her tears. She couldn't cry! Not there and especially not in front of him! She compressed her lips and waged an internal battle with her feelings. Why couldn't she hate him? It would be so much easier that way. But she didn't hate him. She liked him, dammit!

Libby was in such turmoil that at first she did not hear him speak. The instant his fingers touched the cotton fabric over her shoulder, she whirled, gasping. His brows drew down in displeasure at her reaction and he removed his hand. "You don't have to act like you can't stand my touch," he growled. "I don't hate you. I've never hated a woman in my life and I'm certainly not going to start now." And then he smiled slightly. "Besides, you're too beautiful and vulnerable to hate, Doctor. Let's get one thing straight, shall we? Above everything else, I admire honesty. The people who live in the mountains come by it naturally. We don't play games. Sometimes we say things that hurt others, but basically our intent cannot be misconstrued. You were born in the city and grew up where games are played to give and take what you want. Out here you'll get nowhere with that kind of screwed-up diplomacy. You started to ask me questions because you wanted something else of me. All you had to do was ask the real question straight out."

Her brown eyes darkened with pain as she held his steady gaze. Anger and humiliation flooded her and she snapped, "I'm hardly 'vulnerable,' as you put it, at age twenty-nine, Mr. Wagner!"

He shifted the Jeep into higher gear range as they began to pick up speed over the flat dirt road that stretched toward a small group of office trailers in the distance. "Call me Dan," he said, the hardness gone from his tone. It wasn't a command but a request. "I called you vulnerable because every emotion registers so clearly in your golden eyes. You're transparent. That's what I like about you. You can't hide a thing."

She didn't know what to do or say. His voice was suddenly caring, and that threw her even more.

"So, what do they call you at the office? Elizabeth? Betty?" he asked.

"No, Libby," she answered, her voice toneless.

He nodded, his eyes narrowing as if he were thinking about it. Finally he murmured, "That fits you. It's not a weak name, but it isn't a totally independent one either. A nice blend of feminity and strength."

She stared at him, her brows knitting. "What?" she asked.

"Names. Haven't you ever rolled a name off your tongue and noticed that it sounded strong, weak, soft or whatever?" He looked at her for a moment and then returned his gaze to the road.

"N-no, I can't say I have," she answered tentatively, thinking about the concept. She was amazed at the way he looked at the world.

"What was your ex-husband's name?"

Libby sat there for a second, saying the name to herself. Then a small smile edged her mouth. "Harold."

She began to laugh and he joined her. The tension eased between them as she sat back, enjoying the shared moment. Dan's eyes were softer now, and she marveled at the azure intensity of them.

"I'll refrain from making any observations about that name," he intoned dryly.

Libby managed a quiet laugh. "Yes, I think you should. I've probably covered most of them myself."

"How long did it last?"

Suddenly she didn't mind answering his questions. "Five years. About three too long, if you want the truth," she admitted.

"You've been free for a couple of years, then?"

"Yes, two years."

"Like being single, Libby?"

She shivered inwardly as he spoke her name, his voice husky. It sounded incredibly beautiful. "Most of the time, yes," she answered. "Sometimes . . ." She shrugged her shoulders. "It gets lonely."

Dan pulled the Jeep to a halt at the first trailer. The office had once been white, but now it was coated with a thick coat of yellow dust. He switched off the engine, leaning back and turning his gaze to her. His eyes seemed to drink in each facet of her face, and Libby experienced a frightening thrill and a sense of danger about his frank perusal. Finally he turned away and climbed out.

"Well, three weeks in these mountains are either going to make you feel loneliness like never before or a wonderful sense of contentment. I don't know which."

She slid out the door, glad that she had worn her casual shoes as the dust settled on the top of them. Eagerly she looked around at the mountains that embraced the valley. The vivid blue of the spruces mingled with the darker color of evergreens. She spotted a small stand of white birch halfway up on a mountain opposite the road down which they had come. Everywhere the colors seemed vibrant, alive. It was as though the forest were inviting her to reach out, touch and enjoy. Looking across the hood at Dan, she grinned. "Somehow I think I'm going to love it."

3

Long into the evening Libby worked on the business at hand in the command trailer. Large topical maps of the state land-grant area lay sprawled out over roughly hewn work desks as they went over the details of the coming exploration. Dan glanced at his watch and then over at her. She stood at his shoulder, elbows planted on the map, a notebook in front of her with scribbled notes in it.

"It's nearly eleven o'clock," he said.

Libby's eyebrows moved up in surprise. "Already?" Where had the time flown? She stood, suddenly finding that she had been in one position far too long. She pressed her fingers against the small of her back, arching to ease the tension in her muscles. "I guess time goes by quickly when you're having fun," she murmured, picking up the notebook and closing it.

He snorted, rolling down his sleeves. The trailer had

grown cold and he walked over to a stool, dragging his denim jacket off of it. "I don't exactly call this fun," he growled. "A lot of time is going to be wasted because of the damn licensing demands."

"Modern-day chess game, I'm afraid," she responded, meeting his gaze. "I know you don't like games. Now I can understand why you were so angry when you came to my office."

"I'm still angry and I still don't think this is necessary."

She leaned over, picking up her newly purchased coat, which had an inner lining of goose down. In one of Dan's brief letters he had included a list of items she should buy before coming to the mountains. She was grateful now for his instructions. "I wonder if I'll ever get used to being unessential," she commented dryly, suppressing a smile.

Dan walked to the door, opening it for her. "Lady, as far as I'm concerned, these next weeks will be like a vacation. I play tour guide and you do the work. Come on, let's get you bedded down for the night."

Libby stepped past him, barely brushing against him as she slipped through the narrow door. She was wildly aware of the heat radiating from his body. It was as if he were a rock that had been warmed by the sun all day and now, in the darkness, gave off the heat in return. She took the steps one at a time and stood at the bottom, watching Dan come down. Her attention was drawn to the sky, and a gasp of pleasure broke from her lips.

"Oh," she said softly, turning to catch the panoramic view above them.

"What?" Dan halted at her shoulder, looking down at her.

"The sky," she whispered in reverence. "Look at the

stars! They're so *close!*" She raised her arm, fingers extended upward. "I'd almost swear I could touch them from here. Isn't it beautiful?"

Libby felt a thrill. The stars hung like scintillating crystals on a blue-black velvet background. The shadowy shapes of the mountains were black silhouettes against the sky, adding a sense of grandeur to the scene before her.

"What I'm looking at is beautiful," Dan returned huskily. He felt pleasure course through his body, taking delight in her discovery of a world he loved fiercely. Dan gave Libby a quizzical look: Was his imagination playing games on him? She looked like an ancient Celtic druidess instead of a city woman. Her darkly golden hair paled beneath the starlight, an almost incandescent glow touching the untamed tendrils that framed her ethereal features. He had to stop himself from reaching out to see if Libby was real or a figment of his imagination.

She was too enthralled to catch the inflection in his words. "I've never seen stars like this before! Oh, they never look like this in San Francisco," she bubbled.

"You are a child," he mused quite seriously.

Libby turned, lips parted, eyes wide and luminous. Her heart thudded as she saw the undisguised hunger and intensity in his look. She swallowed, suddenly very shy, lowering her gaze. The silence lengthened tensely between them. Finally, as if realizing her discomfort, Dan said, "The reason why the stars look bigger and brighter here is because of the elevation and the lack of pollution." And then he added, "I can't believe a doctor of biology would get so excited about this."

Libby gave him a wicked smile. "I suppose you think

we only jump up and down when we look at microbes through a microscope?"

He grinned, reaching out and capturing her arm. His fingers closed firmly about her elbow, leading her around the end of the trailer. "My contact with the biological field has been, let's say, kept to the bedroom level, not the lab level."

She was thankful for the darkness because it hid the blush staining her cheek over his comment. "I don't know if I'm ever going to get used to your honesty," she admitted.

He stopped at the door of the third trailer and opened it. "Most city folks don't get along with mountain people." Giving her a half-smile, he gestured toward the opened door. "There's an extra bedroom on the right. That'll be yours for tonight. If you want to wash up, you can use the shower first. Just be sure to conserve the water if you can. We have a small heater and it runs out of hot water easily."

Libby gave him a stunned look. "This is your trailer?"

"The company's," he corrected. "Go on in."

Shrugging, she entered the small, confined trailer. It was sparsely furnished with only the essentials, the linoleum floor well worn by time and many footsteps. After the desire she had seen in his eyes as he had looked at her, Libby wasn't sure about staying there. But she had no choice and quickly accepted the reality of the situation. And a quick warm shower relaxed her to the point that when she fell into bed, she dropped soundly to sleep.

* * *

She awoke slowly, vaguely aware of the warmth of a hand against her shoulder. Moaning softly, Libby turned onto her back, her hair spilling across her shoulders. "Libby, it's time to get up," Dan called. He gave her another, more insistent shake. "Come on, city girl, let's get moving."

He had stood over her for a few moments before awakening her. Libby's hair was a golden frame around her head. Dan fought a strong urge to run his lean fingers through it, to see if it was indeed as silken as it appeared. He was transfixed by the guileless quality of Libby's face as she slept. Without the business facade it was the face of an innocent woman-child. A wild, wishful urge filled Dan. Wouldn't it be wonderful if Libby were his woman and they were simply taking a long hike in the wilderness to share the joy of the forest? He sighed heavily, frowning. How could she attract him that way? Dan knew that Libby Stapleton was touching him on many levels. Suddenly he didn't feel as threatened by her credentials. And it made him breath a sigh of relief, because despite everything he was drawn to her.

Dan removed his hand from her shoulder and she missed his strong, warm touch. Barely lifting her lashes, she looked through them. Dan stood above her, hands resting loosely on his narrow hips, a lazy curve to his mouth as he watched her. Rubbing her face with her hands, she mumbled, "W-what time is it?"

"Five-thirty in the morning."

"Uhh, that's impossible: I just fell asleep," she murmured, her voice husky.

He smiled, reaching down and caressing the crown of

her head. "You have beautiful hair. Come on, Rapunzel, I've got hot coffee on."

Libby stumbled blindly out into the glare of the kitchen, dressed in jeans, a long-sleeved blue shirt and her hiking boots. Her hair, still uncombed, curled naturally about her oval face, making her look more like a young girl of twenty than a woman of twenty-nine. Dan stood against the sink, a cup balanced in one hand.

"Here," he offered, "it has cream and sugar in it."

Mumbling her thanks, Libby took it and sat down at the table, one hand against her head, closing her eyes. "My God, do we have to get up this early every day?"

"You'll get used to it."

Sipping the coffee cautiously, she muttered, "I doubt it." Very little registered on her groggy mind during that first half hour. Libby was aware of the delicious smell of bacon frying and of bread being toasted. Dan placed before her a plate with three eggs, six pieces of bacon and two large slices of sourdough bread on it.

Libby's mouth dropped open and she gave him a shocked glance as he sat down opposite her with his plate.

"This can't be mine! I've never eaten this much before in my life."

"Eat as much as you can, Libby," he advised between bites. "We're going to be hiking most of today and your body is going to be needing the carbohydrates, believe me. Come on, dig in."

"I'll get fat!"

He gave her a knowing grin. "No you won't. The first week you'll probably lose weight."

Running out of excuses, she picked at the food. "I

don't normally eat breakfast," she confided. "I never have."

"You're not in the city now. The oxygen is sparser because of altitude and you're going to burn up the sugar in your body a hell of a lot faster. You don't have any fat on you to use as excess energy, so you'll get hungry even faster," he promised grimly.

How did he know there was no fat on her body? She shot him a disgruntled look, trying to remember that this outing was not a vacation but work. Somehow she was too excited to consider it work. And despite Dan's warnings, she was anxious to get started and sample the fare that the mountains promised.

As the first rays of the sun slid across the peaks of the range, Dan pulled the Jeep to a halt. Throughout the two-hour drive Libby had listened attentively to his instructions on the gear they must carry. Two large backpacks were in the rear of the Jeep. He seemed pleased that she had worked up to five miles a day in her hiking boots, and she felt a glimmer of pride. Getting out, he laid a map of the region on the top of the dusty hood.

"We'll be taking a logging road from this point to forty miles northwest of here. We're at sixty-five hundred feet now and will be climbing steadily to about seventy-three hundred before we crest that ridge yonder and go down into some of those valleys that hold the mature stands of timber." He glanced over at her. "Ready?"

She nodded, a smile forming on her lips. "Let's do it."

Libby was amazed at the amount of patience he took with her as he fitted the thirty-pound backpack to her body. He stood close, fingers running the length of her shoulder straps and adjusting the hip padding to ensure a snug but comfortable fit. Stepping back, he looked her over critically.

"Well, how does it feel?"

She walked around a little bit. "Fine. Are you sure this thing weighs thirty pounds? It doesn't seem like it."

"It will in a couple of hours," he promised. "Bend over," he instructed, "as if you were tying a shoelace on your boot."

Libby gave him a puzzled look but obeyed his command. The nylon strap at her waist cut into her stomach and she rose quickly, frowning.

"That's what I thought," he muttered, quickly loosening the buckle and easing the strap tension slightly. "Do it again."

This time she did it with ease. She came up smiling. "Feels good."

Dan turned, shrugging into his pack, which seemed a great deal larger and bulkier than her own. "Remember the procedure, because I'm not going to be checking on you every time you put that pack on."

She ignored his derisive tone, too excited about actually beginning the climb up the gentle wooded slope in front of them. Keeping her notebook and pencil handy, she made a few preliminary comments about the immediate area and then tucked it away. She had tied her golden hair back in a ponytail to keep it out of the way. Wispy bangs lay across her forehead, barely brushing her wheat-colored eyebrows.

"Here, another gift for you," he said without preamble. He handed her a red bandana.

"Thanks. What is it for?"

"Put it around your forehead. You'll be working up a sweat real soon." He tied his around his darkly tanned throat and gave her an expectant glance. "Okay, let's get this EPA show on the road."

The morning was young, with sparkling beads of dew clinging to the knee-deep buffalo grass as they walked through it. Libby tried to notice everything surrounding her as they walked at what she thought was a very slow pace. The dew coated her lower legs, the jeans turning a darker blue where the water soaked in. Within twenty minutes they were on the first slope, winding through the trees.

At first she didn't notice her leg muscles tightening. But by the end of the first hour she was gasping slightly for breath, her cheeks blazing with color from the high altitude. She didn't complain, realizing Dan would probably chide her cruelly for being weak and slowing down their pace. The muscles of her calves were protesting already. Resolutely she lowered her head, concentrating on each step.

"Libby."

She half turned as he called her name. Each time he spoke it she shivered involuntarily. It was as if he were a cat licking her skin, making it tingle. She liked the way he said her name and her spirits rose simultaneously.

"Let's take a break," he ordered, finding a smooth granite rock and sitting down.

"I can go on," she answered stubbornly. "I don't intend to hold us up."

He gave her a warm grin, catching her wide brown

eyes. "I know you can, but we have to take it easy the first couple of days or you won't be able to walk at all. Take off your hiking boots and let me look at your feet."

She found a soft spot on the carpet of pine needles, doing as he asked. No longer did she bother to question his motives or reasoning; she trusted him enough to know he wasn't going to hurt her or take advantage of the situation. Pulling off the second wool sock, she stretched out her feet. Grinning, she said, "I washed them this morning, so its safe."

He slid out of his pack and got up, moving to her side. "You do smell good," he agreed, lifting her foot and gently examining the heel. "Like lilacs. It must be your perfume."

Heat stole into her face and she refused to meet his teasing blue eyes. Just the rough touch of his fingers sliding along the surface of her foot sent crazy messages through her body. For one split second Libby found herself wondering what it would be like to be loved by him. His touch was sure, confident, and it was as if he had known her feet were a deliciously sensitive area of her body.

"What's the prognosis, Doctor?" she asked, a hint of teasing in her tone.

Dan released her left foot, handing her the wool socks. "So far, so good. Every time we rest, I want you to pull the boots and look for red spots on your feet. Those are areas where blisters may develop." He patted her slender ankle and then stood. "That's why we call people like you tenderfoots. You haven't yet developed the tougher skin and calluses on certain areas of the foot that you need for extended hiking."

Libby liked his touch and kept her eyes on him while she pulled on the socks and then relaced her boots. "I've had blisters before and they never bothered me," she noted.

Dan shrugged into the pack. "Yes, but you didn't have to walk fifty miles once you got one, either." He pushed a rebellious curl off his forehead. "And I'm not carrying you if you do get one. So be a good hiker and pay attention to what your feet are telling you. Ready?"

"You bet."

By noon Libby's initial excitement had ebbed a great deal. They had broken out of the heavy timber into a small sun-dappled meadow when Dan finally called a halt to eat. She bit back a moan of relief as she shed the pack. The grass was inviting and fragrant, and she flopped down on her back, closing her eyes in sheer bliss. "Oh, God, I feel like my shoulders are on fire," she whispered. The hot sun felt good on her face, the slight breeze cooling the perspiration on her flushed skin.

"You rest," he said. "I'll make us lunch. Are you hungry?"

She barely heard him; she just wanted to drift into the quick nap that her body was begging her to take.

"Libby?"

She roused herself, barely opening her eyes. He crouched down at her side, holding out a small plastic bag of trail mix.

"Is that lunch?"

"Yup. Come on, don't get too comfortable," he prodded. Reaching out, he gripped her upper arm, pulling her into a sitting position. Her hair spilled in pale golden tresses across her shoulders as she sat up. Dan smiled and remained close.

"Your ex-husband ever comment on how beautiful your hair is?" he asked.

Libby was engrossed in the contents of the plastic bag. "What?" she asked, lifting her chin and meeting his azure eyes.

Dan slid his hand down her crown, caressing her hair in a wistful gesture. "A man could go crazy just running his fingers through your hair," he murmured huskily.

Her heart hammered. Finding her voice, she managed to say, "You mean I don't look like a doctor of biology anymore?"

Dan lay down, propping his elbow against his head, eating the trail mix thoughtfully. "No. You deliberately put all that lovely hair into a bun to look more authoritative?"

Libby scooped up a handful of the nuts, raisins and granola, eating them with relish. She gave him a careless smile. "Let's put it this way: Cascade Amalgamated hired me because they needed more women in managerial positions to fulfill the regulations set forth by the government so that they could bid on land leases. I'm afraid that if I walked in with my hair down, I wouldn't look very professional. Personnel would probably have thought I was applying for a secretarial job instead." She smiled fully, her teeth even and white. "I give them what they think they need."

Dan studied her, but it wasn't that piercing look he usually gave her. "And at home do you let down your hair?"

She laughed, peeling back the paper on an energy

candy bar that was coated with carob. "I'll have to be careful how I answer that one!"

He returned the smile, a new look of interest in his blue eyes. "So what do you do on weekends? Surely not lab work."

"I love to go to the ocean and just walk along the beach." She gave a shy shrug of her shoulders. "I love the peace I find there." And then she looked around the quiet meadow nestled within the arms of the tall, silent trees. "And I love it here too," she confided, her voice tinged with newfound respect and awe for the mountains.

"What's this? A city girl falling in love with the country? Are you sure it isn't the rarefied air getting to you, Libby?"

Her brown eyes danced with unspoken happiness as she looked down at him. "Positive. I—" She sighed. "I love the silence. There's such incredible peace here. In a way it's a shame that, in less than a year, timber trucks will be roaring through here with their noisy diesel engines and most of these woods will be chopped down."

"Remember, though," he said softly, "it will all be reseeded and reclaimed. We're harvesting, Libby, not destroying."

She gave a funny little laugh, blushing. "This sounds silly, but I feel like these woods are a cathedral that God has made for us. It seems like desecration in a way."

Dan gave her a long, measuring look. "Are you familiar with the history of the Celts?" he asked slowly, sifting a handful of dry pine needles through his fingers.

"No. . . . I think I've heard something about them. . . ." She shrugged, giving him a shy look. "I was lousy on history, if you want the truth, Dan. Why do you ask?"

"Something you said reminded me of what one Roman historian wrote about the Celts. When the Romans invaded Britain, they found the tribes strongly united by a religious clan known as the druids. They held their religious ceremonies in what they considered sacred groves of trees. The historian went on to say that the druids and druidesses actually communicated with the spirits that inhabited those trees. Later on, some Roman general ordered the groves to be cut down to break the power uniting the clans by destroying the druids' sacred trees. When you said that these woods are like a cathedral and that chopping the timber down was close to desecration, it reminded me of how the druids must have felt when the Romans cut their forests down." He gave her a bashful smile. "History and mythology happen to be my favorite subjects, if you haven't already guessed."

Libby was fascinated with his story, finding herself a mesmerized child sitting at his feet while he spun the myth. "If history had been taught to me the way you've made it sound, I would have loved it," she responded, delighted in finding another facet of Dan Wagner that met with her approval.

Dan grimaced, getting to his feet. "Who knows, maybe you're a druidess reincarnated, coming back to your rightful home."

"You believe in reincarnation?" Another surprise. But then, he was a totally unique man in so many ways. So it really didn't come as that much of a shock to Libby.

He shrugged. "I'll turn the question back on you. Haven't you ever experienced déjà vu? As if you've been in a certain city or country before? Maybe a vivid flash or recollection of an event?"

She thought about it. "Y-yes, I have."

"Haven't you been experiencing one just now? When you started talking about these trees, this forest, your eyes began to shine, Libby." His blue eyes danced. "For a city gal, you sure are at home out here. Think about it," he challenged, offering his hand to her.

Libby looked up, sliding her hand into his, aware of the strength and steadiness of his grip. Once on her feet, she stood dizzyingly close to his body, her heartbeat beginning to pick up. Reluctantly he released her fingers. There was a searching look in his eyes as he scanned her features. Unconsciously her lips parted beneath his hungry gaze; her breathing stopped. An electrical current seemed to pass between them. Their relationship changed in those few seconds, an unspoken need expressed. Libby trembled inwardly at the invitation in his blue gaze. It was as if he had removed the thick protective walls from around himself for those fleeting seconds so that she could sense how he felt toward her.

"Let's go," he urged huskily, and the magic of the moment evaporated like fog that had been struck by the rays of the sun.

4

Sitting close to the small fire, Libby fought to keep her eyes open. There was enough light to finish writing down her comments about the necessary changes that would have to be made to protect the land from the logging. But darkness fell rapidly, and finally she closed the book.

"All done?" Dan inquired, coming back into camp with another armload of wood. He dumped it near the fire and brushed pieces of bark from his sleeves.

"No. I'm so tired that I'm not thinking clearly," she admitted. Glancing at her watch, she groaned. "It's only nine-thirty! I'm used to going to bed around midnight."

He walked over to her pack, releasing the lightweight sleeping bag and spreading it near the fire. "We made ten miles today, so it's no wonder you're feeling a little tired."

Libby rubbed her eyes. "A little? Humph, a lot. I don't

think I even have the strength to go to that small stream and get cleaned up."

Dan gathered a soft cushion of dry pine needles beneath the sleeping bag. Putting a ground mat beneath the bag, he unzipped it and motioned for her to climb in. "You can wash up in the morning. I'd advise you to sleep with your socks and at least a T-shirt on."

"I didn't bring a T-shirt," she began lamely.

"I'll loan you one of mine."

She struggled to her feet, brushing the back of her pants off. Giving him a weary smile, she went over to the bag and flopped down. Unlacing her boots, she placed them near her head. "Thanks for making my bed, Dan." She meant it sincerely, aware that he was a great deal more considerate than she had first thought.

He brought a white T-shirt over to her, placing it in her hands. "I was afraid you were going to keel over on that log and fall asleep," he said.

Libby glanced up at him. He looked so much a part of the vast wilderness, someone who had grown tall and strong within those forests. My mind is playing tricks on me again, she thought, mumbling good night to him. Barely aware of anything because of the exhausting day, Libby slept the minute her head rested against the pine-needle pillow heaped beneath the sleeping bag.

She awoke to the delicious smell of pancakes and coffee. Turning slowly over on her stomach, she opened her eyes. Dan knelt beside the fire, concentrating on his task. He glanced up at her, smiling. "Good morning, sleepy head."

Yawning, Libby mumbled, "What time is it?"

"Six."

The morning was fresh, clean and silent. Libby marveled at the beauty around her. A pair of scolding bluejays flew overhead and then landed in a tamarack nearby, eyeing the food. She wriggled back into her jeans and struggled out of the cotton T-shirt. By the time she was dressed, breakfast was ready. Dan motioned for her to sit on a log he had drawn up and handed her a bowl filled with steaming, savory wheat pancakes.

"There's the maple syrup," he said, pointing to the plastic container on the log.

She inhaled the nutty aroma of the pancakes, her mouth watering. "I'm famished!" she declared.

Joining her on the log with his own bowl, he set the crisply fried bacon between them, giving her a spoon. "That's quite a turnaround for a lady who said yesterday that she didn't eat breakfast."

"From now on," she promised, "I'll never doubt another word you say."

He snorted. "Except on this damn impact planning, right?"

"Right," she agreed. She cut into the pancakes, noticing small dark berries scattered throughout them.

"What are these?" she asked, pointing at them.

"Hmm? Oh, huckleberries. I spotted some bushes down by the stream this morning and figured it was a good addition."

She ate voraciously. Finally, after the meal, she said, "Dan, I don't know whether it's the air or the elevation, but this has got to be the best meal I've ever eaten. It even tops the best restaurants on the Wharf in San Francisco."

He seemed pleased by her compliment. "Just hang around a little while longer, city lady, and I'll have you longing to return to these mountains after you go back to your office."

Libby wrinkled her nose. "The office . . . my job," she said softly. "It all seems like part of another world."

"It is. Maybe in the coming weeks you'll see why I prefer the back country to the cities."

She gave him a searching look. "Dan, why do you dislike cities and people who live in them so much?"

"I think you'll be able to answer that when you go back to San Francisco."

Not satisfied with his answer, she probed more deeply, encouraged by his openness during the last day. He had lost so much of that hard veneer he wore like armor. The mountains had worked some kind of magic on him. Perhaps it was because he was uncomfortable in big cities or dealing with big corporations. "Is it because you think city people play games?" she insisted.

He cradled his bowl and spoon in the palms of his callused hands. "Let's just say that I think people reared in the city forget some of the natural laws that apply to both man and animal. A golden rule, I suppose." His blue eyes met her gaze. "For instance, when you're in my territory, I make it a point to help you with your gear, to give you any information that might be valuable. In the city you can't even stop someone on the street and ask for directions anymore. All you get is a neurotic stare as if you were a mugger. And you can't walk the streets alone at night for fear of rape or robbery." He shook his head. "The only way you get injured out here is if you're blind, deaf or dumb."

Libby saw his point. "You're making me feel ashamed," she said. "But people have to live where there's money to be made. That's why cities exist."

Dan rose, smiling grimly. "Thank God I can have my cake and eat it too. My line of work doesn't require me to go to the city to earn my pay."

Standing, she tossed him a brilliant smile. "The only time you have to go to the city is when the chief biologist from Cascade Amalgamated asks for your presence in her office."

He took her bowl and a small washcloth from a plastic bag. "I didn't find it that painful." And then he added, "Matter of fact, it was a pleasant surprise in one way." A wicked gleam came to his eyes. "I figured I'd be stuck with some old man who was bent over with arthritis and who would gripe every step of the way on our trek. Instead I find a bright, beautiful woman who I'm discovering has a very commendable streak of naturalness still left in her." He halted, holding her startled gaze. "I'm surprised the city hasn't jaded you, Libby."

She tossed her head, laughing. "Dan, you oversimplify things!" She picked up her towel, washcloth and soap from her pack and accompanied him down the gentle incline toward the small but swift-moving creek. "You know," she drawled, "cities aren't monsters, and the people in them aren't evil trolls."

"You certainly aren't."

"Give us a break. You should feel compassion for city dwellers, not disdain."

Dan knelt downstream of her, washing out the bowls. "Now you're overreacting," he accused lightly. "And, believe it or not, I do go into the city every once in a while."

Libby gave him a dramatic look, dipping the washcloth into the icy water. "Whatever for?"

"I occasionally like to see a play or go to hear a symphony." And then he added dryly, "I suppose you thought I was the Hermit of the North Woods?"

She grinned, leaning down and splashing the water against her face. The icy tingle left her skin feeling taut and refreshed. "Good guess, Dan." She was about to tease him about his poor wife, who was probably locked away in some dark little cabin, but decided against it. There was no ring on his left hand, but that didn't mean anything. Suddenly she doubted all of her neat assumptions about Dan Wagner. Was he married? And then she asked herself why it should matter to her if he was. Libby frowned, highly uncomfortable with her shortsightedness, disliking her reaction to the question. She would never knowingly date a married man. She stole a look at Dan. He was so different from the men she had known in her life! And that difference made her feel incredibly exhilarated. He made her happy. That thought alone twisted the knife of loneliness more deeply into her heart. If he was married, she had to destroy those blossoming feelings.

Four miles from camp, Libby called a halt. They had reached the crest of a mountain range. A flowing green carpet of trees met her gaze in every direction. She saw the gleam in Dan's eyes as he stood there, surveying the countryside. Funny, she mused, how they saw the woods in different ways. He saw it in terms of mature trees, wood products and dollar value. She looked upon the forest as an incredibly beautiful cape thrown about the earth's shoulders by nature. One that should not be disturbed.

Unrolling the map and pinning it down with four rocks the size of his hand, Dan called out the coordinates for each mountain. Libby took the binoculars and began to decide what environmental tests and evaluations would have to be initiated to return the forest to its original beauty when the timber had been logged. Hours fled by as they worked in unison. He told her where he would be placing the all-important logging roads and she scribbled down the environmental measures that would have to be taken. More than once he looked over her shoulder and made bitter comments. The actions she was suggesting meant spending more money than had originally been allocated, and that began to create a rift between them.

Over a lunch of trail mix, cold spring water and carob bars, Dan pursued the argument.

"I get the impression that you think I'm going to rape the mountains," he growled, lying on the pine-needle carpet beneath a white fir.

"I don't mean to imply that, Dan," she said. "I know you'll take care. Doug Adams had high praise for you. And I see how much caution you take here on the trail. When we leave a site, it's as if we'd never been there."

He scowled. "As it should be."

Libby tried to lighten his mood. "You remind me of myself when I got defensive about your attacks on city living. I think you're overreacting to my suggestions for this logging operation. It may cost more money my way, but in the long run the environment will be restored quicker and the state guidelines will have been satisfied."

"The damn government and their red tape," he muttered.

"Something we all have to live with," she assured him. "How do you think I feel? I'm wrestling with the federal people on five different projects right now. Sometimes the US forestry regulations are simply preposterous, and I have to gather evidence to change their minds."

One dark eyebrow lifted. "Oh? You mean you defend us poor loggers sometimes instead of attacking us?" he mocked.

She met his gaze unswervingly. "It may come as a surprise, but I often end up in court, defending the company on certain issues."

A wry smile tugged at his mouth. "I suppose Amalgamated is going to hire a contracting company to come in and do this nitpicking impact study?"

"Yes. It will be my responsibility to send out the bid package to the contractors."

He rolled over on his back, tucking his hands beneath his head. "I don't want you to take this personally, Libby, but damn, most of these biologists and botanists go beserk with their studies. They drive me crazy with their uncanny ability to find some lousy bug and proclaim it rare. Then they tell you that because the damn bug occupies only a certain number of square miles, we have to bypass the area because we would be ruining the lousy insect's home." He looked up, his blue eyes stormy. "They don't know compromise. Do you?"

She nodded patiently. "I believe I do."

"Well," he sighed, "we're sure as hell going to find out, aren't we?"

Libby got up, smiling. "For better or worse, we're on this project until its completion," she agreed.

He gave half a laugh, one filled with derision. "Almost as bad as being married to the wrong woman. Instead it's a company."

Her heart leaped in response to his analogy. "Marriage doesn't always end in divorce, you know." She gave a shrug. "Not that I'm one to talk."

He got lightly to his feet, shrugging into his pack.

"These days," he groused, his tone less tense, "it's safer to live with a woman than marry her. Divorces are a dime a dozen."

"You sound bitter," she hedged, walking at his shoulder as they started down into the valley.

Dan pursed his lips. "Maybe," he agreed. "I've seen too many of my friends take the plunge and then get divorced."

"You never did?" Her heart rate rose as she stole a glance up at him.

"I did. But that was a long time ago," he returned, his voice suddenly flat.

Libby's brows drew down into a slight frown. She sensed that the subject was a closed matter between them. She respected his silence, but couldn't help being confused as well as curious.

For the better part of the afternoon they walked down the steep slopes. Toward the foothills it became more rocky, and Libby had her first opportunity to try to properly balance the pack and her body weight on some precarious rock formations. The temperature was intense, the sunlight reflecting off the heated granite. She had tied the red bandana into a headband to stop the sweat from running down into her eyes. Her face was flushed, a sheen of perspiration making it gleam. Dan was slightly ahead of her, tossing directions over his shoulder when necessary. Looking down at her watch, she saw it was almost three-thirty P.M.

Just as she called out to him to stop and take a break, Libby saw movement on a ledge only inches from her left arm. Startled by the quick, sudden movement, she froze just as the hissing of a rattlesnake broke the drowsy afternoon air.

"Libby!"

Her head snapped in Dan's direction as the disturbed rattlesnake coiled itself, ready to strike. Everything happened in slow motion. Or so she thought at the time. Dan's face paled as he heard the rattler and he spun around, holding out his hand to make her freeze. A startled, frightened cry lodged in her throat and automatically she leaped away from the ledge. The footing was unstable and the sudden weight shift of the pack threw her completely off balance. The gray and black rocks rushed up to meet her and at the last second she threw her hands up to protect her head.

Something cool and wet was being dabbed against her face and Libby moaned, weakly lifting her arm. Her eyes fluttered open, momentarily blinded by the brightness of the sun sifting through leaves overhead. She felt Dan's arm tighten around her body for a moment as she regained consciousness.

"Just lie still," he commanded softly.

Libby winced as he placed the cloth against her left temple. "That hurts. . . ." she muttered thickly. How long had she been out? She felt comfortable being supported by his lean, hard body, her head resting against his shoulder. His heart was pounding thunderously in his chest and she began to realize he was frightened or upset by what had taken place. "The snake?"

Dan's mouth thinned. "Dead."

She closed her eyes. "Good."

She licked her dry lips slowly, trying to remember the exact chain of events. Finally she reopened her eyes, struggling to sit up. Her pack was off and she was lying beneath the shade of a scruffy oak tree. Frowning, she realized he must have carried her off the rocky slope. She looked up as if to confirm her unspoken thought.

"How do you feel?" he asked, pouring a bit more water from his canteen onto the cloth. Again he gently dabbed at the cut on her temple, sponging away the blood.

"I—don't know yet. Give me a second. What did I do, cut myself?" she asked, reaching up.

Dan caught her hand. "Don't. I'm going to put some antiseptic on it as soon as I can get the bleeding staunched. It's just a laceration. You were damn lucky you fell back on that pack first and then rolled onto your side," he breathed tensely. "Next time, Libby, don't panic."

Her golden eyes darkened with pain at his reprimand. "I'm sorry. . . ."

"I suppose you're going to cuss me out for killing the

snake. I just upset the ecological balance up on that rock slope."

She winced inwardly at his cutting tone. Why was he being so damn nasty? She closed her eyes, inclining her head forward to stop the aching that radiated outward from the cut. She felt him disengage himself and suddenly felt bereft as he rose.

"Stay here," he ordered tersely. "I'm going back to get your pack. If you feel dizzy, lie down."

A minute later he was back. She sat stiffly as he cleaned her head wound and bandaged it with quick efficiency. His touch was sure and steady. She found it hard not to be affected by his closeness, his face only inches from her own when he placed the antiseptic in the wound. Libby made a face as the stinging sensation spread out, bringing tears to her eyes. Biting her lower lip, she refused to let him see her tears, fighting them back.

"Well, we've pasted you back together again. Let's take the rest of the day off and I'll make camp here."

Libby gave him a stricken look. "I can go on, Dan. Honest."

He got to his knees, putting the medical items back inside a small watertight bag. "If you could see your face, you wouldn't say that. You're pale. Your pulse is jumpy too."

"But I wanted to reach the valley by nightfall and start getting my soil and water samples tomorrow morning. . . ."

He muttered something under his breath and got to his feet. "You sure as hell have a stubborn streak in you," he said. His stern features softened somewhat as he gazed down at her. "Look, you've been a real trouper on this hike so far. I admire your tenacity, but I don't admire anyone who won't listen to what their body is telling them. You can't tell me you don't have a splitting headache."

She avoided his piercing eyes. "I do," she admitted.

"And you want to walk another five or six miles in this heat?" he challenged.

"Will you teach me how you cook in the great outdoors, then?" she asked, hoping to ease the tension between them.

A corner of his mouth lifted. "Sure. You just rest for now. Your pack has the aspirin in it. We'll get a couple of those into you and you'll feel like new," he promised.

The summer evening remained warm, although the intense heat of the day dissipated when the sun went down. The aspirin made her headache magically disappear, and Libby took renewed interest in his ability to cook delicious meals in such rugged surroundings. At his direction she stirred crushed corn flour and warm water, making it into a thick, doughy consistency. He had found some wild blackberries not far away and dropped a handful in, along with some walnuts from his pack.

"I'll put the dough in a pan with a little grease and set it over these coals, and in about twenty minutes we'll have what they call pan bread."

She smiled, finishing the blending and handing the bowl to him. "I'm starved, as usual."

Dan looked up, his eyes seeming to have lost their glitter of anger. "Sure sign of recovery. Seriously, how are you feeling, Libby?"

She colored under his concerned gaze. "Like I've had the wind knocked out of me," she confessed.

"A meal and a good night's sleep ought to put you back into commission for tomorrow." He frowned. "You were damn lucky you didn't get a concussion from that fall. You scared the hell out of me."

"I scared the hell out of myself when I saw that snake, believe me. Next time I'll try to be more watchful around rocky areas," she promised fervently.

With freeze-dried mushroom soup, the pan bread and brown rice cooked in beef bouillon, along with hot cocoa to drink, Dan made her an unforgettable meal. She wolfed down her share of the food, finally leaning back against the tree trunk, the cup of hot chocolate balanced in her hands. Sighing, she closed her eyes, feeling much better. The pleasant clank of pans and dishes was music to her ears as she sipped the steaming liquid. Closing her eyes, Libby drifted off to sleep, her head tipped back against the trunk.

"Libby?" a voice called. "Come on, city lady, it's time for you to go to sleep."

She moaned, feeling Dan's strong fingers on her shoulder. Weariness was dragging her back into the realm of badly needed rest.

"Lib?"

She moved her head, mumbling something unintelligible. Arms slid around her shoulders and beneath her legs, and she felt like a feather wafting in a breeze. Vaguely aware that Dan had picked her up, she gave no real protest, relaxing against his strong, warm body. His heady male fragrance entered her nostrils as she rested her head against his shoulder. She was only half conscious as he gently tucked her in. And then his fingers caressed the top of her head in a stroking motion, and Libby gave in to the demands of her exhausted body.

In the early morning hours her sleep turned to fragmented bits of nightmare about the rattlesnake. She had seen a snake only two times before in her life, and that was as a very young child. Snakes simply did not exist on the streets of San Francisco or at Half Moon Bay, where she often spent her weekends. Her vivid imagination carried the incident even further as the snake struck at her, his jaws open and venom dripping from his yellowish fangs when he lunged toward her bare, sunburned arm.

Libby jerked awake, screaming. For several seconds she was disoriented, bathed in the horror of the nightmare. A small whimper escaped from her as she buried her head in her perspiring hands. Then strong, lean arms were there, encircling her, holding her protectively.

"It's all right," Dan soothed huskily, stroking her hair gently, drawing her against his body.

"Oh, Dan . . ." she cried.

"You're trembling. Sshhh, honey, you're safe. It was just a bad dream," he reassured her.

Libby hid her face against his bare chest, unaware of the dark hair beneath her cheek. Tears squeezed from between her tightly shut eyelids as she tried to shake the vision of the rattler. Dan's fingers kneaded her tense neck and shoulder muscles in an effort to get her to relax. Finally she stopped trembling, but she remained in his embrace, needing the security he offered.

Libby felt her heart pounding in her breast and

consciously tried to control her fear. "I—I'm sorry," she gulped thickly.

Dan leaned over, his fingers brushing the tears from her cheeks. "Don't be. I would have been surprised if you hadn't gotten at least one bad dream out of it, Libby."

The night was cool, as it always was in the mountains, but his body seemed to radiate heat like the sun itself. "Every time I close my eyes, all I see is that horrible snake!"

He gave her a small squeeze. "It's too early to get up, Libby; you're going to have to try to get back to sleep."

She hated being childish about it. "I feel so stupid," she whispered. "I kept thinking the snake was in my sleeping bag." She shivered violently.

"Easy, honey," he soothed. He drew away, studying her intently. "You are frightened, aren't you?"

"I—I feel so foolish, Dan. I'm sorry. Like I'm falling apart inside and—" She sobbed, no longer able to hold back the tears. "I don't mean to be a pain to work with," she blurted out unsteadily.

He drew her close. "Delayed reaction," he provided grimly. "Will you be all right here by yourself for a moment?"

Libby had wrapped her arms tightly around her drawn-up legs. "Well—yes. . . . Why?"

He rose and was quickly swallowed up by the pitch darkness. Confused, Libby remained still, trying to control the trembling in her body. Dan reappeared at her side and knelt, unzipping her bag and then opening it up. "Come on," he coaxed, "lie down here beside me."

She gave him a startled, wide-eyed look. He managed

a soft smile, pulling her down beside him. "Look, Lib, we both need our rest. I think you'll be able to sleep if I hold you close. We've got a rough day ahead of us tomorrow and we can't afford to keep each other up." He placed his opened sleeping bag over them.

He maneuvered a speechless Libby around so that her back was curved against his body, her head resting against his arm.

At that point she couldn't decide which was more disturbing, the rattler or being thrown unexpectedly into Dan's arms. But as his breathing became regular she realized he was doing it out of practicality. And, more than anything, Dan was practical. That thought soothed her alarm and she felt her shoulders relaxing, the tension melting away.

"Good girl," he whispered huskily, his breath moist against her neck. "Good night, my druidess. You won't have any more bad dreams tonight." His other hand slipped across her T-shirted stomach, resting against her, fitting her perfectly against the frame of his body.

She was safe, and that was all that mattered now. Like a lost kitten, she snuggled against him as exhaustion reclaimed her.

5

〜◦◦◦◦◦◦◦◦◦〜

The sun was shining through the lacy fingers of the oak tree overhead when Libby stirred drowsily. The mouth-watering smell of oatmeal and coffee wafting on the cool morning air brought her to full wakefulness. Bits and pieces of the previous night's incident began to filter into her consciousness as she struggled into a sitting position. Had it been a dream after all? Dan's strong arms about her, holding her close? Libby turned, her lashes lifting to meet the interested gaze of the man who had held her the night before.

"How do you feel?" he asked, his voice husky.

Libby's lips parted and a warming tingle went up her spine. Somewhere in the vagueness of her memory she recalled his mouth moving across her lips. Had it been a dream? Her heart fluttered wildly and she experienced a giddiness that left her breathless. Had Dan kissed her sometime during the night? She held his concerned gaze, trying to gather her scattered thoughts. There was a new tenderness in his blue eyes that morning as he watched her, and Libby found it impossible to speak.

"You still look a little pale," he observed, giving the oatmeal a final stir and then adding bits of dried dates to it. "Want breakfast in bed?" he asked, his mouth pulling into a teasing curve.

Libby ran her fingers through her long, tangled blond hair. "N-no, I'll get dressed. Give me a minute."

She quickly dressed and completed her toilet, hurrying back to the campfire. Dan was sitting on a rock, spooning the oatmeal into two bowls.

"What's your rush?" he asked.

"I just looked at my watch and realized it was eight o'clock."

"Relax, will you? I let you sleep late." He handed her the bowl. "I've been a little rough on you and decided to ease up."

Libby shot him a startled look, sitting down opposite him and pouring them each a cup of coffee. "What do you mean? Haven't I been keeping a fast enough pace for you?"

He shrugged, dipping into the oatmeal. "You're a tenderfoot. I keep forgetting that because you're taking to hiking so naturally." He gave her an intense, searching look. "You have stamina, Libby, and I tend to take advantage of people who possess that trait. Yesterday's accident shouldn't have happened. I should have been at your side instead of assuming you could get across that difficult area."

"Thanks for the backhanded compliment," she murmured. "And you're right: I love hiking. No one's more surprised than I am." She gave him a careless grin, which he returned.

"You have a headache this morning?"

"No, it's just a little tender," she responded. A new bond had been built between them, and Libby wasn't sure when it had happened or why. "Thanks for baby-sitting me. I feel more than a little embarrassed over my performance last night."

Dan got to his feet and scraped a second helping of oatmeal into his bowl. He sat down again, his blue eyes dark and unreadable. "I've known enough women to know the difference between a performance and actual fear," he drawled. "And that wasn't a performance."

Libby blushed. "I feel like a child out here sometimes, Dan," she admitted softly. "The wilderness is so vast and rugged. I feel lost in it." She lifted her eyes, meeting his azure gaze. "And in some respects I feel like a child around you because I know so little about hiking and camping. My reaction last night totally frightened me." She managed a broken smile. "There are no snakes in San Francisco."

Dan grinned. "It's a good thing, lady, or you'd be in my arms every night as a consequence. Not that that's a bad idea. . . . I rather enjoyed it myself. Do you realize you snore?"

Libby straightened up. "What?"

He laughed. "I'm only teasing. You're a soft, warm kitten, Lib. Come on, quit looking so devastated and vulnerable. Let's pack and get going; we've got some tough climbing to do today."

She considered his candid words as she gathered up

her things. They sent a shaft of pleasure through her and she found herself smiling. She was determined to be a better hiker that day. If she wanted Dan's cooperation on this project, she would have to extend herself and earn his respect. It would be the only way that she could effectively deal with him and make the project a success for everyone involved.

They worked their way down through a narrow valley filled with knee-high grass and flowers, moving up toward the timberline into a vast rocky region. Sweat was trickling freely down her temples when Dan called a halt at noon. The sun was hot, the wind brisk and the sky an intense cerulean blue, matching the color of Dan's eyes. Libby took the red bandana off her forehead, wiping her face and neck, her gaze sweeping across the ridgeline towering above them. A smile pulled at her lips and she rested her hands against her hips, feeling the exhilaration of challenging the mountain.

The wind playfully blew strands of her golden hair against her face and she pulled them away. Dan stood above her, watching her with renewed intensity. He motioned toward the incline.

"If I didn't know better, I'd think you're excited about climbing this mountain."

She laughed, meeting his curious expression. "You're right, I am." Shrugging, she admitted, "Right now I feel like I'm on top of the world and can conquer anything. Does that sound like a typical tenderfoot statement?"

Dan returned her smile, leaning over and capturing her hand. "Come on, lady, let's use the shade of this poor old spruce over here and eat lunch before we go on."

A new excitement surged within her as she ate the trail

mix in silence. Libby was beginning to understand Dan's love for the mountains and the forest that spread out below them like a velvet green cape. It was her third day and she realized that her body was adjusting beautifully to the high altitude and responding to the demanding exercise. Looking at her arms, she realized that she had become tan. Her fingernails, once long, had been broken or chipped. Digging in her pack, she decided to cut all the rest and get it over with.

Dan was lying against his pack, his eyes half closed.

"You like it out here, don't you?"

Libby looked up. "Does it surprise you—a city girl suddenly turning country?"

"A little."

She grinned. "A lot, I think."

"You're looking good. Usually by the third day a tenderfoot is either giving up or shifting into high gear and getting the feel for it. Looks like you've surpassed even me. I can see the excitement in your eyes, Libby. I never realized until just now how clear your emotions are in your eyes and face." He gave her a tender look. "Never give up that quality. It becomes you."

She stared, at a loss for words. His last statement caressed her like a lover's hand. There was a hunger burning deeply within his eyes and she swallowed against a lump, losing her gaiety. A primal need surged through her as she sat facing him. God, had one night in his arms shaken loose all her carefully controlled passions? Sleeping with a man was heaven to her, and she had missed it more than anything else since her divorce. And last night had torn down the walls she'd put up to protect herself. Nervously Libby stood, shrugging into her pack and belting up. "Sometimes I'd like to be less readable," she groused. "Harold read every thought I was thinking and it got me into a lot of trouble."

Dan reached out, pulling her around to face him. He rested his hands against her shoulders. His brows were drawn downward, eyes unreadable as he studied her upturned face. "Your openness will never get you into trouble with me."

Libby's heart leaped wildly as he reached out, his thumb gently tracing the natural curve of her cheek, coming to rest beneath her chin. Pleasurable tingles leaped like electricity through her tense body at his knowing touch. He searched her face for a long moment, as if memorizing each detail and nuance of her features.

"You're a beautiful golden druidess, Libby," he breathed huskily. "So alive . . . so damned enticing and yet so dangerous. . . ." His mouth descended, grazing her parting lips in a feather-light kiss.

Her senses reeled at the touch of his mouth, and she felt his hand steadying her, pulling her toward the hardness of his body. His masculine scent was a heady perfume to her senses, and Libby closed her eyes and swayed against him. The second time his mouth came down strongly against her lips, parting them, teasing her until an explosion of fire roared to life within her. A soft moan escaped from her throat as she felt his hand sliding downward, caressing the curve of her breast. Finally, after what seemed a delicious eternity, he pulled away, his eyes turbulent. They stood inches apart, staring at one another, stunned in the aftermath of what their kiss had ignited. Libby pushed herself away from him, her hand planted against his broad chest. "Please," she whispered tremulously, "we can't . . . shouldn't . . ."

His hand gripped her arm as he studied her with a new, ruthless intensity. "Why not?" he rasped thickly.

Confused, needing him and at the same time feeling frightened of her own violent reaction, Libby freed herself from his grasp. He was relentless, like a mountain lion stalking his prey, and she felt helpless when he was that close. Moving away even more, she turned, her eyes reflecting her internal anguish. "We have a job to do," she stumbled, "and—"

He walked toward her ominously. "Now you're playing a game," he growled softly. "Play it with other men, Libby, but don't play it with me. Or is it because you're suddenly repelled by the fact that I'm not from the same side of the tracks as you are?"

Stunned by his brutal question, she turned, her cheeks blazing with color. He let her go and she blindly started up the smooth granite slope. After a few minutes Dan caught up with her, gripping her arm and pulling her to a halt. Libby turned around and faced him, partly out of fear and partly out of anger.

"From here on until we top this ridge, we'll keep a rope between us," Dan ordered, pulling one from his pack. She stood stiffly as he adjusted the snap on her belt. His closeness was nearly unbearable in her present mood. As he released the rope, which was now fastened securely to her body, Libby stepped away.

For a moment they stared at one another like adversaries. Libby met the coolness of his gaze defiantly, lifting her chin. He sighed, resting all his weight on one leg and throwing both hands on his hips. "I'm not going to have you mad as a hornet when we start this climb, because I've got to have your cooperation, Libby."

She had unconsciously clenched her fists at her sides. "You accused me of playing a game with you back there. Well . . . it wasn't! Since you're so demanding about total honesty, why don't you tell me whether you're divorced or married? I make it a point never to get involved with married men. It's stupid and it isn't worth the risk."

Dan gave her a measuring stare. "Is that the only reason why you pushed me away?" he demanded coldly.

"Yes."

His eyes became opaque and unreadable. "Doesn't it bother you that I'm just a logger? A blue-collar worker who earns a living wielding a choke chain or a saw?"

She gave him a confused look. "What are you talking about? Why should someone's job have anything to do with anything?" she demanded, exasperation tingeing her voice.

Dan shook his head disbelievingly. "You're either a very clever liar or you really do believe what you're saying."

Libby lifted her chin defiantly, anger spilling over in her words. "I have never let something like that stand in the way of friendship or love. Why should it?"

"It does for a lot of women," he said stonily.

Her nostrils flared in fury. "Damn! I'm not most women!"

A slow, unsure grin tugged at his mouth. "That's an

understatement. I gather from your reaction that you've had a bad experience with a married man."

She frowned. "Yes, if you must know, I did. Isn't it obvious?"

"You're not a risk-taker?" he probed.

Her heart was pounding furiously in her breast. "I take calculated risks," she hurled back, some of the fury draining from her voice.

"That's wise," he agreed.

Libby gave him a perplexed look, unsure of where the conversation was going. "You still haven't answered my question," she reminded him tartly.

He gathered up the coil of rope and fastened it in place as he walked up to her. He halted, giving her a searching look for a long moment. "Would it make you feel better to know I'm divorced?" he demanded, an ironic glint in his eyes. "Does that make me a better risk?" he taunted softly.

Libby colored instantly, unable to meet his inquiring eyes. "You could be the only man left in the world and you'd be the world's greatest risk!" she countered, seeing his coolness.

A grin spread across his craggy features. "Touché, my druidess. Come on, we've got three hours of hard work in front of us."

Miffed, she followed him, listening carefully to his directions on where and how to place her feet in the toeholds provided by crevices in the rock. The hours sped by and she ran through their conversation several times, analyzing it. What kind of woman had married him? And what were the circumstances of the divorce?

Had she been unable to meet his demands? Somehow Dan Wagner seemed inflexible to her. He always seemed to have a chip on his shoulder about his job, and that perplexed her. She had found out one thing of interest though: He liked risks. Not just small ones, but big ones. And he respected her reactions to his questioning. A silly grin pulled at her lips, and she felt slightly better about this enigma of a man who climbed the mountain with her.

It was late afternoon when they reached the top of the yellow-ocher ridge. The sunny day had suddenly clouded up, and towering cumulus clouds rose in threatening shapes on the horizon. Libby sat on a rock opposite Dan, sharing a drink of water from his canteen. She felt incredibly happy up there where the wind never seemed to die down. Dan shrugged out of his pack.

"Time for a break, Libby."

"Too bad; I was really getting into the swing of it."

He looked up, breaking a candy bar in half and giving her some of it. "You did very well."

She tossed him a light smile. "We risk-takers are up to it," she retorted, and bit into the sweet chocolate.

He stood looking over the lower mountains and the thousands of acres of mature timber below them. "You are a definite risk-taker," he agreed, turning and catching her gaze.

Libby joined him. "Only in certain ways," she corrected him, returning that lazy smile. "Isn't this beautiful?" she asked, her voice filled with newfound reverence.

"Almost as beautiful as you are," he agreed.

"Flattery will get you nowhere."

"Really? Is that why you're blushing?"

"Sunburn."

Dan's eyes crinkled with amusement. "Do you always turn compliments aside, Libby?"

She smiled. "Sometimes. Especially yours."

He slowly unhooked the rope from his belt and walked over, unsnapping it from hers. He met her wide-eyed stare. "Afraid of me?" he asked huskily, their faces no more than a few inches apart.

She didn't feel very fearless that close to him, but she forced a smile. "Don't try to scare me with your macho charisma, Dan Wagner. It won't work."

"I didn't get that impression last night or earlier this afternoon," he hinted.

Her heart fluttered briefly in her chest. She was playing a dangerous game with him. Either he was ignorant of her ploy or just patiently biding his time to call her hand. "Just to keep things 'honest' between us, Dan, I don't go around falling into the arms of every man I meet. You included. The circumstances last night were unique." She compressed her lips, watching him through her wheat-colored lashes. He frightened her in many ways—ways that left her feeling unsure of herself emotionally. The last thing she wanted was a one-night stand. It wasn't worth the emotional risk, and despite the permissiveness of the times, Libby needed more than a fling.

She grimaced inwardly as she set about helping Dan find enough wood to fuel a small fire. Dan was the kind of man who got exactly what he went after. She trembled, scooping up several more twigs and bringing them back to where Dan knelt, coaxing the fire to life behind a rocky shelter. She had seen that measuring look in his eye when he watched her, and it created butterflies in her stomach and a flutter in her heart. At twenty-nine she was well past such high school reactions. Yet, Dan excited her in dangerous and unknown ways. She sat back against the sun-warmed rocks, watching his progress.

"Do you always get what you want?" she asked softly.

His head snapped up, his eyes narrowing on her features. "What?"

Libby rested her chin against her palms. "You strike me as a man who has gotten everything he ever went after. Is that true?"

He frowned, returning to the fire. "What gave you that idea?"

She laughed. "Everything about you! I mean, you came stalking into my office and turned my world upside down."

He sat back, placing a larger branch on the small fire. "I've gotten everything I went after, but sometimes I didn't realize the cost involved until after I got it," he growled.

"Don't tell me you leaped before you looked?"

"That was when I was younger," he countered. "At my age I look very carefully before I go after my next goal."

"Mmm, my feelings exactly. So tell me about yourself, Dan."

He gave her a dark, hooded stare before getting to his feet. "You're being awfully chatty all of a sudden." He reached into his pack, bringing out food for their early dinner.

"Would you prefer if I talked to the rocks or maybe the wind?" she returned tartly, confused by his sudden withdrawal.

"You'd better be looking at that building cumulus,

lady. Because in about an hour we're going to be in for one hell of a storm. Instead of talking, why don't you start exploring this ridge and see if there are any niches where we can hide to escape the brunt of it." He gave her a tight smile. "Unless you want to stand out here and risk getting struck by about a million volts of electricity."

Libby glanced at him and then turned, looking at the approaching storm front. All along the horizon the black, roiling mass of clouds had tripled in size and height and were bearing down on them. "We never get thunderstorms in San Francisco," she murmured, awed by the force that nature had assembled.

"Don't look so worried. You'll be guaranteed an electrical display that will never be equalled by any Fourth of July."

Libby walked past him and he reached out, gripping her wrist.

"Hey," he growled, "now be careful up here. One wrong step and you'll be hurtling down the side of this thing. I don't want to lose you."

Her arm tingled wildly at his touch, and she felt relieved as he withdrew his hand. "I would have thought you'd be glad to get rid of me," she taunted lightly. "After all, if I'm gone, the environmental plans will surely be tabled for a while."

He grinned tightly. "Just be careful, Druidess."

Libby's smile faded beneath his blue gaze. The huskiness in his voice showed his concern, and that affected her. Watching her step, she walked along the top of the ridge with the high-gusting winds at her back. It took her nearly half an hour to find a suitable shelter. Smiling triumphantly, Libby returned, suddenly famished. The sky was darkening rapidly and every few minutes she looked up at the threatening clouds.

Dan invited her to sit down with him, using the giant boulder as a windbreak. He handed her a cup of steaming split-pea soup, pan bread with onions and a healthy portion of scrambled eggs. She dropped down beside him, smiling her thanks.

"Well, did you find anything?"

"You'll be proud of me," she said between bites. "I found a small cave a short distance from here."

"You didn't go inside it, did you?"

Frowning at his question, she mumbled, "No. Why?"

He swore softly, shaking his head. "At least you have some sense. There could easily be a wild animal in there, that's why."

Stung by his lack of faith in her common sense, Libby remained silent, eating quickly. Dan was done first and he efficently put out the small campfire and packed his utensils. The wind was whipping with increasing fury across the ridge, and Libby felt an uneasiness deep inside her. She looked around at the ugly clouds coming nearer. Already she could see wicked forks of lightning striking jaggedly down at the forest.

"Let's get going, Lib," he ordered, watching the storm. He helped her stand, slipping the straps of the pack over her shoulders. Gripping her hand, he said, "Stick close: This wind is gusting a good fifty miles an hour."

She didn't need another warning, clenching his hand in a death grip. The fury of the gusts increased as they carefully made their way toward the area of the cave. She looked over her shoulder, her eyes widening.

"Look!" she called, pointing up at the sky.

Dan halted, looking upward. "Damn," he snarled. His grip tightened on her hand. "We're in for a hell of a storm. If we hurry, we can make that cave before it hits."

They ran as quickly as they could, Libby leading the way. When they reached the cave Dan turned, gently pushing her against the wall outside the dark hole. "You stay right here."

"What are you going to do?" she yelled above the rising wind.

"Make sure there are no animals in there. Watch how it's done." He picked up several fist-size rocks and carefully moved to the lip of the cave, throwing each one into the darkness. Shrugging out of his pack, he removed the flashlight, getting down on his hands and knees and searching the darkness more thoroughly.

The storm hit with an unparalleled fury, and Libby was caught off-guard by its sudden attack. Lightning danced around the ridge, and thunder caromed off the sides of the cliffs. The rain struck furiously and she lifted her hands to her face, protecting her eyes from the onslaught. The noise, the crackle of electricity and the howl of the wind drowned out Dan's voice. Within seconds she was drenched to the skin by the storm. Blinded, she groped forward as she heard Dan's second call, her hand stretched outward.

The rocks were slippery and she took two steps forward. At that moment the wind whipped sharply in a twisting pattern, catching her and knocking her off-balance. A cry broke from her lips as she threw out both hands to stop herself from falling. Just as suddenly Dan's arms were there, halting her fall. Libby gasped, regaining her feet and allowing herself to be dragged forward.

Getting down on her hands and knees, she felt the scrape of the rocks against her flesh. Dan pulled the pack off her back and she lay on her side, panting for breath. She felt his hand tremble as he pushed her wet hair off her face.

"Libby? You all right? Answer me. . . ."

She gulped a steadying breath. "Fine. . . . Just . . . give me a second. . . ."

Another bolt of lightning flashed in front of the cave and Libby cringed, burying her head in her arms. The cave was cold, but she shivered from fright as well as the sudden drop in temperature.

"Come here," he ordered gruffly.

There was barely enough room to sit up, and Libby crawled into his waiting arms, collapsing against his hard body. He pulled a blanket around her shoulders, holding her tightly against him.

Her heart thumped erratically as she clung to him, regaining her sense of equilibrium. With her head against his chest she could hear his heart beating solidly. Slowly she began to relax within the confines of his grip, finally feeling a corner of safety from the savage storm.

"God, you scared me out there. What the hell happened?" he said harshly.

Libby swallowed painfully. "The wind . . . it threw me off-balance. I'm sorry, Dan."

He caressed her face, his hand rough and callused against her smooth skin. "Lady, you damn near fell off that ledge out there. Do you know how far down—?"

"Don't," she rasped, squeezing her eyes shut. "I said I was sorry, dammit!"

He gave her a brief hug. "I'm sorry too. I shouldn't be

yelling at you when you're trembling like a leaf in my arms. I was worried, that's all."

She didn't want to leave the safety of his arms or the warmth of his reassuring body. But at the same time he infuriated her. She opened her eyes, staring off into the darkness, which was at intervals punctuated by lightning. "One minute you're growling at me like an old bear, and the next . . ." Libby felt him laugh. She closed her eyes as he caressed her cheek more gently this time.

"I told you before," he murmured. "I don't want to lose you, but you seem bent on disappearing. If you don't want me around, say so. But don't go jumping off cliffs to prove it."

She sat up, breaking the contact between them, real anger going through her. "Don't flatter yourself by thinking I'd jump off a cliff to get your attention," she snapped, jerking the blanket around her more tightly.

In a flash of lightning she saw him sitting back, watching her, a self-satisfied grin on his lips. Her nostrils flared and she muttered, "I've never met anyone with such an incredible ego before!"

"Compliments will get you nowhere. Now calm down, will you? It's going to be a long night, and whether you like it or not, we're stuck with one another for the next ten hours or so. Want to call a truce so we can both get some sleep, or are you going to lie awake, spitting and clawing?"

6

Petulantly Libby fumbled in the darkness, waiting for lightning flashes in order to locate her gear. There was very little room to work, and their bodies brushed together more than once as they struggled to unroll their sleeping bags. The temperature dropped alarmingly without warning and Libby began to shiver once again. She stubbornly said nothing, clamping down on her chattering teeth. But too soon she could no longer endure it and began groping for her jacket, which was tucked away in her pack.

"What's wrong?" Dan wanted to know.

"I'm—cold," she chattered.

He reached out, pulling her into his arms. "You need to get out of those wet clothes."

Libby struggled, alarmed by her sensual reaction to Dan's warm body. "I'll just get my jacket—"

Dan held back an exasperated sigh. "Get out of the clothes, Libby. It's the only thing that will help. Here, I'll zip the two bags together and you can snuggle down between them."

She was frightened by her own attraction to Dan. The wind howled into the entrance, and Libby's teeth chattered so badly that she couldn't even answer him. She heard him swear softly and felt his arms capture her.

"Come here before you freeze to death," he growled, pulling the one sleeping bag over the top of both of them. Systematically he began to release the buttons on her blouse.

Horrified, Libby shoved his hands away. "Wh-what are you doing!" she protested, stammering.

"Trying to get you out of these wet clothes!" he growled. "Now, just relax, I'm not going to rape you, for God's sake!"

His fingers were like an exquisite brand upon her cool flesh as he stripped off the soaked blouse. Expertly he released the hook on the bra. Her heart beat wildly in her chest as he pressed her upper body against him. She clung to him, needing his warmth above anything else.

"Just lie here and try to relax," he breathed against her ear. "You're damn near hypothermic."

Libby closed her eyes, resting her head on his shoulder, grateful for his continuing warmth. "What's—hypo—" she stuttered.

"It's when your body temperature drops to a dangerous level. If we don't stabilize your body, you can go into shock." He ran his callused hand across her naked back in small circles, rubbing her skin briskly. "Usually people who fall into mountain lakes get it," he explained, his voice a roughened whisper. "But it's been ninety degrees out there today, and the temperature has dropped to close to freezing in less than an hour. That kind of drastic change can bring on hypothermia too."

"Mmm," she mumbled, finally feeling some semblance of heat returning to her shoulders, hips and back, where he continued to briskly rub her skin. She began to relax in his arms, feeling a subtle euphoria. Libby laid her head on his arm as he worked to bring blood back into her chilled legs and feet. By the time he'd finished, the storm had abated in its initial fury. Still, the wind continued to howl across the ridge, making strange, eerie noises she had never heard before.

Libby was aware of the textured material of his jeans against her lower body, and the softer flannel of his shirt against her breasts. She inhaled the smell of his maleness and a soft smile curved her lips as she buried herself more deeply into his welcoming embrace.

Finally Dan lay down beside her, keeping both his arms around her. "There," he whispered, "you should be warmer now."

"I am," she returned softly. "Thank you."

Dan reached out, stroking her damp unbound hair, delighting in the silken texture of it. Libby responded to his hand on her head, nuzzling upward. She felt his breathing change, become more shallow. Opening her eyes, she could barely see the outline of his craggy features. Her heart opened spontaneously as he met her gaze. How could she ever have thought Dan was cold and unfeeling? Being in his arms, having been protected and cared for by him, she knew he was a gentle man. The toughness was only skin deep. Hesitantly she reached out, her long, slender fingers tracing the rugged planes of his face. She heard him groan, felt his arms tighten about her.

"Libby," he growled thickly, "don't if you—"

She placed her fingers across his strong mouth, a newly ignited fire flaming brightly within her aching body. "Love me, Dan," she whispered throatily, meeting his burning blue gaze.

He hesitated. "I don't want to hurt you, Libby," he murmured, taking her fingers, kissing each of them gently. His eyes became readable, and Libby saw pain in their depths. Without realizing it, she responded to his vulnerability, pressing her body against him, tilting her head up to meet his descending mouth.

The world came to a halt around them as his mouth grazed her waiting lips. A shiver of pleasure coursed through her as his mouth pressed more insistently, parting her lips, demanding entrance. His tongue moved with delicate slowness, exploring her moistness, drawing her into a blazing inferno of barely contained desire. Her breath was hot and shallow as his hand roved the length of her neck and shoulder, slowly circling her tautened breasts, teasing her. He dragged his mouth from her lips, leaning down, capturing a hardened nipple between his teeth.

She arched, moaning as Dan slid his hand between her thighs. Mindlessly she reached out to touch him as he was touching her, wanting to give him as much pleasure as she was receiving. Their kisses became torrid as she unbuttoned his shirt, running her fingers across the magnificent expanse of his torso and chest. Dan groaned as she released his jeans, boldly slipping her hand beneath the material. He tensed beside her, growling her name, wrapping the long strands of her hair in his fist, gently drawing her head back. He rose above her, his eyes filled with a dark intensity.

Dan stared down at her, amazed and pleased by her ability to love him just as fiercely as he was loving her. Despite Libby's fragile Swedish beauty there was a courageous heart in her gently curved body. Lovingly he leaned down, tasting her parted, eager lips. She was unafraid to meet him on his own ground, where it counted. He gloried in that fact, wanting to please her more than he had pleased any woman before. She was responsive, welcoming, sharing, teasing and sensual all at the same time. It dizzied his senses and he lost himself in a sharing that rarely happened unless there was a great deal more than physical desire between two people. He traced her wet, throbbing lips with his tongue and stroked the velvet of her inner thigh with his hand, feeling her tense.

"Dan," she whispered breathlessly, "please . . . take me . . ." she begged.

A tenderness came into his eyes as he slid his hand beneath her slender waist, pulling her beneath him. She was like quicksilver, her undulating form sending a raging, unchecked fire through his hardened body. Gently he entered her moist, welcoming depths, watching her eyes widen with pleasure and surprise over their union. A groan escaped him as he plunged more deeply, feeling her response with unabashed jubilation. They were one. They were eagles in free flight, wheeling and diving with one another. He felt her tense, a cry of joy escaping her parted lips. His heart seemed to burst with an incredible joy he had never before experienced. His own explosive release hurtled him to the edges of the universe. Dan lay on his side, drawing Libby protectively against him.

Libby gulped, feeling a trickle of sweat between her breasts as she rested weakly against Dan. Her breathing was fast and erratic, her eyes closed. "Oh, Dan," she whispered raggedly.

He caressed her hair. "You're something else, my druidess," he said thickly. "Something else. . . ."

She slept afterward, feeling safe within his strong, masculine arms. It was only at dawn that Libby awoke, realizing that Dan was already awake and studying her in the gray twilight. He had risen on one arm and was studying her with tender interest when she roused herself, rolling onto her back. As she lifted her thick wheat-colored lashes Libby saw his features above her. A soft, vulnerable smile fled across her well-kissed lips, lips that still tingled from his branding mouth.

"Good morning," she whispered.

Dan returned the smile. "It is," he agreed, his voice husky.

Libby stared up at him. His face was peaceful now. Gone was the harshness she had seen there before. In his own way he was devastatingly handsome. No longer were there lines on his brow or at the corners of his eyes. Instead she saw a flame of tenderness that made her heart blossom in silent happiness. They had shared something far more than just a meeting of bodies. She closed her eyes as he stroked her hair, responding openly to his gentle touch.

"I've been watching you sleep," he began quietly. "I never realized until now just how beautiful you really are." He gave her a wistful smile. "There's a cleanness about you, Libby. Something I can't quite put my finger on . . . a naturalness. You proved that last night by the way you loved me. You weren't inhibited. You were free and giving, like the spirit of the these woods. . . ." He shrugged, embarrassed by his own words. "You really are a part of the forest." He stared out of the entrance of the cave at the green carpet of trees far below them. He returned his attention to her, caressing her upturned face. "My druidess."

Libby shivered pleasurably beneath his touch and his softly spoken words. "Before I say thank you for all those wonderful compliments, maybe you had better fill me in on Celtic druidesses."

"Well," he began, running his fingers down the expanse of her golden arm, "the Celts believed that each tree contained a nature spirit in it. A soul, so to speak. They treated trees like living beings, considering their age a mark of wisdom. The druids would 'talk' to these trees. The druidesses were women who acted as oracles and worked with their male counterparts in the sacred forests. Even to this day there is a special mystical quality to those areas in Britain."

Libby responded to the magical quality in his voice. She was mesmerized by his husky tone. "You've seen the groves?"

He nodded. "I've been where they used to stand. I never believed all those Celtic myths until I walked through the area." He frowned, searching for the right words. "I felt—different. It wasn't anything I can explain. It was just a feeling."

Libby rose, tucking the blanket around her breasts, loving the warmth of their intimate conversation. "I sense that you feel uncomfortable with just a 'feeling,'" she noted.

A careless smile pulled at his mouth as he drew the long golden strands of her hair across her shoulders, watching them curl against her. "I've been accused of being insensitive as hell in the past," he replied. "Maybe I am. I don't know. I was raised to see black and white, to be practical in every circumstance. Feelings are intangible. You can't prove them, weigh or measure them."

Libby reached out, capturing his hand, bringing it to her lips and resting her cheek against the roughened, hairy skin. "You aren't insensitive," she protested. "Just the opposite, Dan. I—I've never had a man make such wonderful love with me." She gravely met his surprised eyes. "Never. You're one of a kind."

His fingers brushed her chin. "So are you. Sure you aren't a figment of my imagination?"

Libby laughed with him. This was the other side of Dan Wagner, a side that she could helplessly fall in love with. Love? Libby felt her heart race upon that discovery. Suddenly unsure of the emotions that Dan had released within her, Libby gently steered the conversation back to him.

"I keep hearing you say negative things about yourself," she said. "You aren't insensitive, and your lack of education doesn't take away from your intelligence, Dan. Who made you believe that? You're a man who has obviously traveled around the world and become familiar with many cultures. Your experience more than makes up for your lack of formal schooling."

Dan's face grew quiet, his eyes veiled and distant-looking. "You don't miss much, do you, Lib?"

She swallowed hard. "I care enough about you and about myself to ask. You're the one who said honesty is the best policy."

He looked around the cave, finding his pack and pulling some of the breakfast items from it. "And it's one of the many qualities I like about you, Lib." He sighed heavily, turning to meet her gaze. "My growing-up years weren't very pretty. Suffice it to say that my father beat me and my mother with regularity until the state legally protected us from him. My mother died a year later and I went from one foster home to the next." He grimaced, recalling those painful memories. "I was a rebel without a cause, Libby. I hated. It was easy to hate and be hated. I had a real chip on my shoulder until I was seventeen."

She blinked once, her heart wrenching with anguish at the rough tone she heard in Dan's voice. "And what happened when you were seventeen?"

He drew the skillet from the pack, his mouth pursed. "I started stealing. Thank God a cop caught me red-handed. He could have put me in jail, but he didn't. Instead Hank took me up to a forestry camp and threw me into the world I've been a part of ever since. I guess he figured a little bit of hard work and sweat would get the kinks out of my system. He was right." Dan gave her a strange look. "I know you can't imagine what it was like, Libby. And I don't want your pity. I got enough of that wasted emotion from my first set of foster parents."

Libby's honey-brown eyes glittered dangerously with unshed tears. No wonder Dan was so defensive! And yet, despite the horror of his youth, he had turned into an incredibly sensitive, caring human being. Swallowing against the tears, Libby reached out, capturing his hand. "Never my pity, Dan. But you have my understanding and compassion."

He rose to his knees, his bulk filling the cave. "Funny," he mused, "I'd expect that from you, Lib. You wear your heart on your sleeve, but there's plenty of courage there, too." He leaned over, placing a tender kiss on her lips. Setting the utensil down, he took her back into his arms. There was something beautiful in her expression as he brought her to his body. He didn't want to get up and leave her. No, his impulse was to make love with her again, this time with the slowness and tenderness she deserved. Last night had been a new awakening for them both. . . . He buried his head against the silken strands of her hair, inhaling her fragrant scent.

"I need you, Lib," he whispered thickly. Another part of him was shocked by that admission. He had never needed a woman since—He blocked that episode out of his mind, drowning himself in the present and Libby's welcoming arms.

Tears glittered threateningly in her brown eyes as she cradled his face between her hands. She felt the prickly growth of beard beneath her fingertips as she tilted her face upward . . . upward to meet his descending male mouth.

The kiss shattered her composure, his mouth moving with galvanizing slowness across her waiting lips. He groaned, gripping her shoulders. "Now I'm going to love you like I first wanted to," he whispered against her yielding lips. Hungrily he nibbled at her lower lip, tracing each corner of her mouth with his tongue, delighting in her total response to his teasing. He gently forced her back down on the sleeping bag, caressing her cheek. A soft smile lingered on his mouth as he undressed, casting his clothes off to one side.

The morning was chilly and he worried about her catching a cold. Moving beneath the warming folds of the sleeping bag, he brought her back into his arms. She was a Celtic legend come to life. Her hair was in disarray, the sun's rays slanting in, backlighting her head, giving her an unearthly look that made the moment even more magical. Her eyes . . . God, her eyes were alive with joy as she reached up, her fingers trailing down his broad chest. He shivered beneath her light touch, shutting his eyes as he felt her hand trailing downward below his waist, stroking his sinewy thigh. "Lib . . ." he growled, gripping her. His body was on fire, a throbbing, out-of-control fire for her once again. He exercised iron-willed control over himself, wanting to give her as much pleasure as he experienced beneath her hands and body. Leaning down, he traced the beautiful half-moon curve of her breast. The nipples were hard beneath his onslaught, and he delighted in hearing her moan as she pressed her body insistently against him in response. Taking the nipple into his mouth, he tugged on it gently, feeling her fingers digging deeply into his shoulders. Yes, he thought in the fiery haze that bound them hotly to one another, feel the pleasure, Libby. Feel it and know that I've never wanted to please anyone more than you. . . .

She was trembling, her eyes wide, begging as he

placed a series of kisses down her stomach to the silken carpet of gold below it. She smelled incredibly wonderful, completely feminine, a woman of unquenchable spirit and aching, demanding passion. He gently slid his hand between her beautifully curved thighs, thighs that were sleekly taut, without a trace of excess fat. Her flesh was silken and warm to his questing fingers as he sought to bring her to the edge of desire. She melted beneath his exploration, calling his name, pressing herself to him. She was his. The begging look in her eyes told him that as he moved above her. The pleasure that flowed through him while giving her that kind of joy left him dazed in its wake. He slid his hand beneath her hips, feeling her arch in welcome to his forward thrust. A groan came from deep within him as he felt her body welcome him. She was his. . . . That thought tore down yet another barrier that he had so angrily erected more than a decade earlier.

She was giving, taking, falling into a wonderful rhythm of passion, carrying them beyond any limit he had ever experienced. His heart nearly exploded as he felt her tense beneath him. He pulled her closer to him, increasing the height of her pleasure as she climaxed. He saw tears slide from beneath her tightly shut lids and he kissed them away. Moments later he released the control he had exercised over himself, taking utter satisfaction in the heated depths of her.

Afterward, Dan kissed her damp forehead, holding her close to him. He placed his hand between her breasts, feeling the wildly erratic beat of her heart. She groggily lifted her lashes, gazing up at him. "You take my breath away," she whispered softly.

"I can feel it," he murmured, placing several small

kisses on her eyes, nose and finally her beautifully shaped lips.

Libby snuggled close, spent, exhausted, deliriously happy and satiated all at once. "I've never been loved by anyone like this," she admitted in a wispy tone.

"Me neither," he admitted. His heart melted as he watched the golden flame in her eyes burning with the fire of life. Flames of passion, he told himself. He raised his hand, smoothing several tendrils of damp hair from her temple. "You bring out the best in me, Lib," he told her softly. "When you love unselfishly, I have no other choice but to give in return."

Libby caressed his cheek, delighting in the prickly touch of a day's growth of beard. "You're unselfish, Dan Wagner. You've never been selfish as far as I know."

He frowned, giving her a pat on her rear. "That's not what some women have said," he returned. Unwillingly he looked at his watch. "As much as I want to spend the rest of the day here with you, we've got to get moving."

Libby nodded. "I know." There was a note of regret in her voice.

He tucked her back in after he had eased out from between the covers and dressed. "I'll put the coffee on. Come on out when you're ready."

After she had dressed, Libby crawled carefully out of the cave on her bruised knees. The rosy hue of dawn made the sky look as if it had been washed clean by the storm the night before. Several colors ranging from the palest pink to a dark crimson stained the early-morning sky in striking array. Libby stood there silently viewing the incredibly beautiful spectacle. She felt Dan come to her side.

Slipping his arm around her shoulder, he murmured, "Now you can see why cavemen worshiped the sun as a god. Beautiful, isn't it?"

She rested against his length, a feeling of contentment rushing through her. "I don't have the words," she said in a hushed tone, listening to the clear songs of several birds that were heralding the rise of the sun.

Dan gazed down at her, thinking he did not have words to describe how he felt about Libby. No longer was she an executive in a white smock, spouting biology like some professor. She was a warm, loving woman whose fierce love of life matched his own. "Come on," he urged, "coffee's on and I'm making us a special breakfast of pancakes with dried fruit."

Retaining a grip on his hand, Libby wordlessly fell into step at his side, watching where she placed her booted feet. No matter where she looked, the world was clean, silent and inspiring. Never had she experienced such sensations in her walled-up city apartment. How much had she missed by never exploring nature? Suddenly Libby was grateful for Dan's unexpected intrusion in her life. Hunkering down beside him near the small fire, she poured their coffee. She took pleasure in watching him mix the batter for the pancakes. He glanced over at her.

"Why the hell did your ex-husband leave you?"

Libby sipped her coffee, holding his interested gaze. "Harry couldn't cope with a successful wife at his side, if you want the real reason."

"And the other reason?" he prompted.

Libby felt no reservations about confiding in Dan. She knew instinctively that her secret thoughts and feelings were safe with him. "He had an affair."

Dan's brows drew downward in silent anger. "The man had to be a complete idiot, then," he growled, pouring the batter into the heated and greased skillet.

"I think he wanted out, Dan. Maybe he thought that flaunting an affair in front of me would make it easier. I don't know."

"Did you love him, Lib?"

She hesitated. "I was young when I married Harry. Looking back on it, I think it was infatuation. Something that turns your head and senses all at the same time. I wasn't thinking straight."

A grin edged his mouth as he expertly flipped a large pancake. "I didn't think straight once myself," he admitted ruefully.

"Yeah?" she teased softly.

"Yeah. Only it looks like you walked away from your marriage without too many scars, and I didn't."

"Were children involved?" Libby asked.

Dan put the large pancake in her bowl, handing her the syrup and a fork. "No, thank God, there weren't." There was a wistful note in his voice. "I wanted them, but Sheila didn't. It's probably just as well. It ended up in a messy divorce."

"I'm sorry," Libby whispered, seeing pain in the depths of his blue eyes. She sensed something else but couldn't quite put a finger on it. "I'm not going to say this very well, Dan, but . . ."

He looked up. "It's all right. One thing I found out a long time ago is that it's better to talk than to hold things inside yourself."

"I just feel a sense of loss or unhappiness around you," she said unsurely. "You came out of a rotten family situation, then reached out to a woman you probably loved, only to be struck at again. I've got to think you're running scared from emotional commitments because of that."

The smile he gave her bordered on a grimace. "You're right on all counts, Lib. I've been divorced for ten years and I'm still gun-shy." He wanted to add, "Until now," but it just wouldn't come out. There was something about Libby that made him want to surmount the walls he had erected to protect his battered heart from a serious relationship with a woman.

She resumed slowly eating the delicious pancake. "I don't blame you," she said softly, her eyes revealing other unspoken emotions. Did that include her too? She imagined it did. Libby began to question why she had made love with Dan. She had never, in all her life, become so quickly involved. She couldn't explain the magnetism that existed between them. Later, as they hiked, she would try to examine her feelings more closely.

"Was it your ex-wife who made you insecure about your background?" she wanted to know.

Dan nodded, sliding his pancake into the awaiting bowl. He put the skillet aside and joined Libby on the fallen log. "Sheila's form of punishment was insidious. She knew how to hit a man's ego." He shook his head, as if shaking off bad memories. "Let's get on to happier topics," he suggested between bites of the pancake.

Libby took a deep breath, agreeing. There was an intensity about Dan Wagner that had been very evident during their lovemaking the night before. Someday, Libby realized, that intensity might bring her pain. But the privilege of knowing the real Dan Wagner was worth the risk. The price was high, but so were the rewards; Libby decided to throw caution to the wind.

As the sun rose above the horizon they packed everything and began to map the surrounding country with the use of a forestry chart. They worked easily together, and the hours sped by.

Over a well-earned lunch of trail mix, orange juice and dried figs, Dan questioned her about her past. "Are your parents alive?" he asked.

"Yes. Dad's a doctor in San Francisco and my mom teaches biology at a community college nearby."

"Brothers or sisters?"

Libby shook her head. "No, just me. The spoiled brat."

Dan smiled. "Were you a brat growing up?"

"Not really. I was a good little girl who did what her parents expected. That's why I ended up in biology. Like mother, like daughter, I suppose."

"You sound like you're not sure you made the right decision."

Shrugging, Libby said, "Looking back on it, Dan, I would have wished for more latitude in making choices."

"Then you didn't grow up wanting to be a bug doctor?" he teased.

She smiled sadly. "No, not really."

"What, then?"

Libby saw the teasing warmth in his eyes and responded to it. "Maybe a lady sailor crossing the seven seas—or a veterinarian, because I love animals so much."

"Ah, the adventuress in you is coming out again." His

blue eyes danced with devilry. "You might have become a lady pirate or maybe a tamer of wild animals. You have a way with animals, you know," he said, his voice dropping.

Libby blushed beautifully, avoiding his gaze, knowing full well that he was referring to their lovemaking. She raised her chin defiantly. "Or maybe I'd want to have become a forest ranger or something."

Dan's laughter rang across the ridge, clear, resonant and sensually disturbing to her. She felt like so much workable clay in his presence; it was as if she had no control over herself.

"Well, if the last couple of days are any indication of your feelings for the woods," Dan said, becoming serious, "maybe you had better think of changing professions. You didn't seem very happy cooped up in that plush San Francisco office you have to inhabit."

"You met me after I had survived a horrendous week, Dan. I was at my wit's end by the time you arrived."

He grinned boyishly. "And I didn't help matters, did I?"

She shot him a direct look. "You know you didn't. But I can't blame you under the circumstances."

He continued to grin. "I'm glad I asked you out to dinner, even though we were both tired."

"You have got nerve, Dan Wagner!" she declared, rising and dusting off her jeans.

He stood. "Listen, even then I was intrigued with the lady who wore that white smock. I wanted to know the real woman in there."

"And now you do."

Dan took the mug from her fingers. "Not quite," he hedged. "I'm beginning to know. Discovering someone like you is like walking into Shangri-la."

She blushed again. "Come on!"

"Just take the compliment, Lib," he ordered.

Making a mock curtsey, Libby laughed with Dan. "You should have been Sir Galahad," she accused, walking with him back to the map.

"Only if you'll be my lady," he answered seriously, catching and holding her wide brown eyes. "All you need is a long dress and you'd fit the fair-damsel image."

She giggled, kneeling down near the map and picking up her notebook. "You don't need a thing to fit the image of a knight in shining armor, believe me," she returned earnestly.

Dan grimaced, bending down next to her. "I'm a tarnished knight at best, with a bad record, Lib. Don't be so quick to put me on any pedestals. I fall off mighty easy."

7

Libby watched as Dan stowed the last of her luggage aboard the light Cessna airplane. Where had three of the most marvelous weeks of her life gone? Even she noted the difference in herself since she'd trekked through the wilderness with Dan. She had arrived looking pale and thin. She had come out of the Salmon River Mountains darkly tanned, her flesh firmed up, a new confidence radiating from her and a new light of enthusiasm in her golden eyes. And Dan Wagner had been responsible for it.

A sadness enveloped her as she met Dan's blue-eyed gaze. How different the man was now from the way he had been the first time she met him at the Challis airport. There was a boyish quality about him now. No longer did he keep that tough facade around him. Her body still tingled from their lovemaking earlier that morning. They had arrived back the night before, sleeping in his double bed in the mobile home that served as his residence at the construction site.

Dan walked up to her, his face becoming unreadable. He led her around to the other side of the plane while the pilot climbed into the cockpit. "Give me a call to let me know you arrived home safely, Lib," he ordered. His grip tightened on her arm and he gently swung her around to face him. He saw the pain of their parting in her guileless eyes, eyes that he could drown and lose himself in forever. They had agreed not to kiss good-bye in front of the other employees.

"I will," Libby murmured, swallowing back tears.

Dan gave her a reassuring smile. "It's been a fantastic three weeks. Three of the best weeks of my life."

"Mine too. . . ."

Dan compressed his lips. "Go on," he said softly, giving her a small shove forward, "before I lose my ironclad control and kiss you anyway."

She nodded miserably, turning away and climbing up into the cockpit. When would she see Dan again? Her job did not normally include weekly or even monthly trips to a job site. Libby felt her heart wrenching in anguish as she lifted her hand in farewell, the plane rapidly taxiing away from the ramp, leaving Dan standing there all alone. Well, she had asked for it. She had thrown caution and her heart to the winds of fate. As a result, she had three of the most beautiful weeks of her life to keep as memories. But she wanted more. Much more. And she knew without a doubt that she had fallen hopelessly in love with Dan.

The flight back was long, increasing her loneliness

because there was nothing else she could do but think
. . . think of Dan, of their laughter, their love and their
nonstop happiness. Had it all been part of the mighty
forest's spell? Had they both been enchanted by the
druids and druidesses Dan liked to talk about? She loved
to lie on her stomach near the campfire each night as he
spun story after story about those mystical beings who
had walked the earth at an earlier time in history. Or was
Dan a druid himself?

Libby had watched in amazement as wild animals
walked within a stone's throw of Dan. He would seat her
on the ground near him and they would patiently wait
until small herds of whitetail deer passed by within fifty
feet of them. Libby became an enthralled child as he
showed her how to feed the shy chipmunks who crept
near their camp to steal a tidbit or two. And she had
gasped in utter delight when he pointed out two bald
eagles frolicking thousands of feet in the blue sky above
them. Dan had opened up a whole new world to her and
she had rejoiced in it.

Returning to her apartment was like going back to a
vacuum. Libby had been home no more than fifteen
minutes when she called Dan. Relief soared through her
as she heard his husky, quiet voice on the other end of
the phone.

"Was it a boring trip back?" he asked.

"Terribly lonely," she confessed. Libby tried to behave
in an adult manner, but she felt like a love-struck
teen-ager.

"Maybe that will make you come back here, then," he
suggested.

Her heart skipped several beats and she gripped the phone harder. "I miss the forest already," she admitted.

Dan laughed gently. "What about me?" he teased.

Libby's spirits rose momentarily. "I miss you more than everything else, Dan."

There was silence for a moment and she closed her eyes, thinking she had said the wrong thing. "That's good to hear, Lib," he answered seriously. "Listen, you get in a tub of hot water and soak. And when you get back to work, I hope you won't mind a few calls every week from a lonely forester."

Her eyes shone with happiness. "No . . . I'd love it, Dan," she whispered, close to tears. Oh, God, how she missed him! After hanging up, she loitered in a tub of fragrant water, seriously examining her career, goals and personal life. Libby came out of the tub much later with no clear answers except that the weeks spent in the forest had helped her discover a new part of herself that she wanted to explore. Sighing, she slipped into a comfortable lounging robe and went to the kitchen to make herself something to eat, even though she had no appetite.

Doug Adams sauntered casually into Libby's office. She looked up between the piles of projects that were assembled at various places on her desk.

"Well, two weeks back and you look just as beleaguered as when you left," he said, offering her a smile.

Two weeks, Libby thought, disgruntled. It feels more like two years. She put her pen down, giving her attention to Doug. "With two court cases pending, an angry biologist on my hands and twenty phone calls to return, I don't know why you'd say that, Doug," she returned.

He frowned. "Plenty of problems came up when you were gone," he agreed unhappily. "You got most of your defense together for those court appearances?"

Libby leashed her growing sense of frustration. If it hadn't been for Dan's calls during the week, she wondered if she would have survived. How many times had she paced the confines of her sterile office, wishing for a backpack, a pair of hiking boots and the opportunity to tramp across some high-country meadow? "Yes, Betty's typing up the final notes, Doug," she responded, harried.

"Maybe you need another assistant," Doug said seriously.

Libby glanced up at him, pushing a stray strand of blond hair behind her ear. As always, she wore her thick golden mane in a chignon at the nape of her neck. "I think you're right. The job is growing by leaps and bounds, Doug."

He rubbed his jaw, nodding. "Okay, I'll see what I can do for you." He started toward the door. "Oh, by the way, who's low bidder on that Sleeping Deer Mountain lease?"

She searched through another stack of papers, drawing one sheet out. "You mean the company that will be doing the ecological study?"

"Yes."

"Pershing Associates. Why?"

"They sending out their head bug man, Trevor Bates?" Libby shrugged. "I don't know."

Doug grimaced. "If they do, fur is going to fly between

119

Bates and Dan Wagner. They're enemies from way back."

She groaned, rolling her eyes upward. "That's just great!"

"Why don't you put in a diplomatic phone call to Pershing and find out who's being assigned to Sleeping Deer Mountain. Maybe we can keep Dan happy and out of our hair. I hate like hell to ruffle his feathers."

Libby quelled a smile, recalling Dan's heavy-handed methods when he chose to attack. "Yes, I know what you mean. Okay, I'll call Pershing this afternoon."

It was almost four-thirty that day when Betty came flying into her office. "Dr. Stapleton!"

Libby raised her eyes from the document she was working on. She frowned, hearing the distress in her secretary's voice. "What is it, Betty?"

"Mr. Wagner is on the phone and he is furious! He's asking to talk to Mr. Adams. What should I do? He sounds like he's ready to kill anybody he can get his hands on."

Libby drew in a deep breath, glancing at her phone. "I'll take the call, Betty. Just switch it in here." What now? Getting up, Libby quietly shut her office door and returned to her desk in time to pick up the ringing phone.

"Dan? This is Libby. What's wrong?" she asked.

"Libby?" his voice was hard. "I wanted to talk to Adams."

"I asked Betty to switch your call to me."

She heard Dan take a deep breath, his voice coming

across the line in a cold chill. "I didn't want this falling at your door, Libby. I want to bounce this one off Adams. It's his damn fault, anyway."

"What are you talking about?" she demanded, exasperated.

"Trevor Bates, that's who. Dammit, that idiotic bug man is assigned to my new lease. I won't have it, Lib. The man's a fanatic who makes up things and throws plans off schedule without batting an eye. That bastard screwed up perfectly usable timber land for me seven years ago and I damn near killed him then. I won't have him on a project of mine again."

"Wait," she begged, making an effort to remain calm and patient. She had never heard Dan so agitated and it upset her. "Tell me about Bates."

"He's an entomologist with Pershing Associates. He's a little guy with Coke bottles for glasses. I don't see how he can count anything with his eyes. The last time we had to work together, Bates went into the interior on an extended study and said he found some damn rare insect that needed protecting. He pulled a hundred thousand acres of prime timber off the lease and my operation wound up in the red, Libby. It was the one and only time I lost money for the company. If he gets assigned to Sleeping Deer Mountain, he'll do the same damn thing."

Libby fumbled through the papers, finding the low-bid assignment. Reading closer, she saw that Bates had already been assigned to Dan's lease. "Look," she said, "I'll see what I can do. Doug was already in here and he mentioned that he hoped Bates wasn't assigned to the lease. Let me get back to you on this, Dan."

His voice suddenly softened, wrenching at her heart. "I'm sorry, Lib. I didn't want to bother you with this. I know it's not your fault that it happened."

She blinked, wanting badly to be near him. "It's all right. It's just one more thing. . . ."

"You've got me worried, Lib. You're sounding more tired as the weeks go by. Are they working you to death up there?"

Her voice cracked. "It's pretty bad. More than anything, I miss you, Dan. I wish we could see one another. . . ."

"I've been doing a lot of thinking, Lib," he began huskily. "About you. About me. I think we need to sit down face-to-face and discuss some things. Look, I'm trying to pull free here, but we're gearing up and—"

"It's all right," she whispered, loving the velvety sound of his voice. "Just knowing that you care and want to come is enough for right now, Dan. We're both under the gun right now with our jobs. Maybe in a month or two, when things settle down . . ."

"Realistically it's not possible at this point," he agreed. "But that doesn't stop me from wishing you were here with me from the time I wake up in the morning until I go to bed at night."

"Do you know how good that sounds?" she asked softly. "I miss you terribly, Dan. I miss the forest. Everything."

He gave a low laugh. "That's the curse of being a druidess, Libby. The call of the wilderness is summoning you home."

"Home," she murmured. "The forest is like a home to me, Dan. I can easily understand why you love it. And I don't blame you for staying there. I want to be there myself. One way or another, I'll come back to Challis," she promised. "Maybe not today, but perhaps for a weekend."

"That's a good idea. I'll be waiting for you, Lib." Dan gave a sardonic laugh. "Hell, you may be here sooner than you think if they drop Bates on me. We damn near got into a fist fight last time, and I feel no compunction about hitting him this time. After what he did to my last lease, he has it coming."

"But did anyone check on Bates's ecological analysis?" Libby asked, perplexed. "Because it's my policy that when a biologist does discover a probable ecological imbalance, I go in and check it out myself so we have some supporting facts. That way we can make a decision based upon two scientists' tests."

"Well, if you can't get Pershing to assign someone else to my lease," Dan growled, "then I know I'll be seeing you within two months. I just have a gut feeling Bates will come up with some damn off-the-wall theory. If I were a masochist, I'd wish for Bates, because then I'd know you'd be coming," he said, a touch of irony tingeing his voice.

Libby smiled warmly. "Truly you are a knight, Mr. Wagner. Only a knight would place himself in the line of fire to rescue a damsel in distress," she teased.

Dan laughed with her. "The only one who will be distressed is Bates," he promised. "Call me when you find out something on this, will you?"

"I will, Dan."

"I miss you, Druidess. And so does my forest."

She closed her eyes, biting down on her lower lip. "You're so special to me, Dan," she admitted, her voice barely audible.

"You're one of a kind Libby," he murmured, "and you've made me do plenty of soul-searching lately." He hesitated. "Like I said, there are things we have to talk about, but I don't want to do it over a phone. We're just going to have to hope that in a month or so we can get away from our jobs and meet."

Libby gave Doug Adams a rueful look. The weekend had crawled by and she had come in early to the office to try to catch up on the mounting workload. On Monday morning Pershing Associates had called to confirm that Bates was the only man available for the Sleeping Deer Mountain lease.

"Dan is going to hit the ceiling," Libby said.

"Don't I know it," Doug groaned, pacing the length of her office. "Dammit!"

"Just how reputable is Bates?" Libby demanded.

"He's thorough, but he's picky and belabors a point when it isn't necessary."

Libby leaned back in her chair, familiar with that kind of biologist. Frequently, when a scientist felt his field of expertise was being questioned, he became adamant and blindly opinionated in order to salve a wounded ego. "Is Bates a stickler for fact or is he just out to support his own theories?" she asked.

Doug shrugged unhappily. "I honestly don't know,

Libby. Bates gave us a hard time a number of years ago, insisting that he'd found some rare insect on our lease lands."

"I know, Dan told me about it."

Adams stopped pacing and looked down at her. "Frankly, Bates should have been questioned on his findings. We never sent in another biologist to check out the site. That's when we decided to hire a company biologist to keep tabs on people like him. Sometimes I think Bates was making a mountain out of a mole-hill."

Libby rose. "Well, if he's one of those types, he won't get away with it this time," she promised grimly.

It was early September, and Libby stood by her office window, looking toward the Bay Area. Two and a half months had passed and she still felt the pull of the mountains in her blood. No matter how hard she worked, she never forgot those glorious weeks spent with Dan in his forest. Turning, she gazed warmly at a lovely bouquet of flowers that sat on her desk. Dan had sent them the day before, reminding her that fall was in full swing and that he missed her greatly. She sauntered over to the vase, touching the golden chrysanthemum petals between her fingers. The phone rang, breaking her daydream.

"Hello?"

"Libby, it's Dan."

Her eyes widened, her heart beginning to pound because of the hardness in his voice. "What's wrong?"

"I'll give you one guess," he said. "Bates."

Her heart sank and Libby said, "Oh, no. . . . What did he find?"

"You aren't going to believe this," Dan continued stormily. "The idiot swears he spotted a California condor up here."

There was dead silence for a moment while Libby digested the statement. California condors were rare and protected by federal laws. Almost extinct, the world's largest bird made its home in California. Finally she managed to squeak, "What?"

"A condor. Bates swears he's been watching a condor for the last week up in the interior near Ridge 256. Libby," Dan said fervently, "he's going to try to order all our machinery out of that section. I've got bulldozers, graders and dump trucks trying to make a road into that area before the first snow falls in late October. I'm on schedule with the road completion date, and I'm not hauling one piece of machinery out of there unless Bates's so-called siting is confirmed." He took a deep breath, then continued. "I've lived most of my life up in these mountains, Libby, and I've never seen a condor. Never! That guy is half blind. How the hell can he see two feet in front of him, much less through a pair of binoculars, looking up at some cliff face where this bird's supposed to be living?"

Libby spent nearly a half hour on the phone with Dan, trying to calm him down. Doug Adams was equally unhappy with Bates's discovery. "Well, I hate to say it, but you're going to have to fly out there and settle this one way or another, Libby," he said. "Damn! I just knew this would happen." He glanced at her. "You'd better get out there tomorrow. If Wagner gets his fingers around Bate's throat, there will be premeditated murder charges to deal with besides this fiasco."

Libby subdued her excitement. "I will," she promised Doug. "I'll have Betty get me a ticket for a flight out tomorrow morning."

8

~~ooooooooooo~~

The sun shone down fiercely on the Challis airport as Dan impatiently watched the small Cessna taxi in from the runway. Libby would be on board. Anger with Bates warred with his happiness at being able to see Libby once again. Had she grown more lovely in her absence? Had she lost the beautiful tan that made her brown eyes look gold and her blond hair almost silver? He put his hands on his hips, catching a glimpse of her as the plane pulled to a stop.

Libby broke into a smile as she carefully stepped down from the plane and into Dan's arms. His welcoming smile created havoc with her heart as she reached out and fell into his strong embrace.

"You look wonderful," he told her, leaning down to capture her parted lips. He pressed his mouth hungrily against her sweet, full lips, tasting her, inhaling her female scent, which mingled with the lilac perfume she always wore. He slid his hand downward, capturing her hip for a moment, pressing her against him, letting her know just how much he had missed her in the intervening months.

Libby eagerly returned his ardent kiss, finally drawing away. Her clear brown eyes were filled with happiness as she surveyed his craggy, sun-weathered features. "Oh, Dan," she whispered tremulously, joy in her voice.

He grinned, giving her a quick hug and reluctantly releasing her. "I like what I see in your eyes, lady. Come on, let's get your luggage and I'll fill you in on the way to the main camp."

She had purposely worn jeans, a lavender-colored scoop-neck T-shirt and sensible shoes. Libby stared at Dan. He looked incredibly virile.

She breathed deeply of the pine, tamarack and fir as they quickly left the small enclave of civilization behind, following the rugged dirt road that wound up through the surrounding hills. Everywhere she looked the mountains blazed with the vibrant oranges, reds and yellows of autumn. She laughed, reaching out and touching Dan's broad shoulder.

"Do you have any idea of how good it is to be back here?"

Dan's eyes crinkled with amusement. "Judging from the look on your face, I think I do. Welcome home, Lib."

"I feel a little guilty, you know," she confided. "Poor Bates is our excuse for finally getting to see one another."

Dan scowled, his brows drawing together in a downward arc. "Bates or no Bates, I had decided before this all broke loose that I was going to fly to San Francisco and kidnap you."

Her lips parted in amazement. "You were?"

Dan nodded, a smile tugging at one corner of his mouth. "Yes, ma'am. I was going to surprise you, but Bates beat me to the punch. Besides, I'd much rather spend our time together here in our forest than in a city."

She loved his words: their forest. She turned, gazing over at Dan, happier than she had ever been in her life.

"Will I be meeting with Mr. Bates when we reach the camp?"

Dan snorted. "No. He refuses to come out of the interior. He's camped up on Ridge 256. All we get are these daily calls from that battery-charged radio he backpacked in with, giving us his position and sketchy reports."

"Why won't he come out?"

Dan shrugged, anger in his eyes. "He says he's got a study under way and won't leave until he's completed it."

"When's that?"

"Who the hell knows? He won't give me an ETA. As a matter of fact, he won't talk to me at all. He'll only talk to Chuck Busch, my foreman. Every time I get on the radio, he breaks off contact." Dan ran his strong fingers through his reddish-brown hair in frustration. "Maybe it's just as well, Libby. Because this time he's gone off his rocker. There's never been a condor this far west. I've seen condors in Peru and deep in the Andes and I know what they look like. Bates ought to stick to counting bugs instead of trying to pretend he's a damned ornithology expert."

Libby curbed a smile. "So I have to go in after him?"

"Correction: You go nowhere alone." He gave her a

sharp glance. "You see how dry the woods are? Take a look around. It's like a tinderbox up here. We haven't gotten sufficient rain this summer and the ground is hard. Green plants that normally survive have died and dried up. We're sitting on a critical fire situation as far as the US Forestry Service is concerned. One good lightning strike will blow this place up like that." He snapped his fingers.

She sobered, looking around. It was true: Even smaller trees were dying, their once green limbs turning brown from lack of the life-giving rain. "You seem to know quite a bit about fires."

Dan grimaced. "I was a smoke jumper for five years, Libby. I've been dropped in on top of just about every kind of forest fire known, including those damn crown fires." He shook his head, his eyes filled with disgust. "I hate crown fires. They're the most common and the worst to control. Usually they start at the top of one tree, and then the fire leaps to the crowns of neighboring trees, spreading with disastrous speed."

Libby stared at him with new interest. She knew little about smoke jumpers and the subject intrigued her. "Tell me about smoke-jumping. This is fascinating. Is there anything you haven't done?" she asked, awe in her voice.

"I'm sure there is. I worked for the US Forest Service from the age of twenty until I was twenty-five. My team and I were equipped with parachutes and special firefighting gear. We'd be dropped far enough ahead of a fire to try to put up a line to stop it. It was grueling physical labor, believe me."

"Why did you quit?"

"Busted up my leg on one drop. I damn near bought

the farm on that one. I was unconscious and had a broken leg. My buddy Dave freed me from a tree, rescuing me just in time. The wind changed direction and the fire came directly at us. He carried me a good mile on his back before a truck picked us up and they got me to the hospital."

Libby digested the account, suddenly grateful that he was no longer in that line of business. "It sounds terribly dangerous," she murmured.

"It is and it isn't. Jumping isn't bad; it's the fire that's always your real enemy. Wind changes or a front coming through and creating different wind directions always makes it difficult to evaluate a forest fire."

Libby shivered, wrapping her arms around herself. "It would be horrible if these mountains caught on fire."

"Happens every year, Libby." There was worry shadowing his eyes. "And right now we're sitting on a powder keg. As much as I personally dislike Bates, I wish to hell he'd fold up his tent and get back into camp until the danger is over. The thunderstorms are on the increase because of the temperature rise that occurs this time of year, and I just have a bad feeling about the whole situation."

"So I can't go in and contact Bates?"

"Yes, you can, but we'll do it together," he explained. He offered her a tender smile. "Ordinarily all I'd do is order one of our choppers to drop you off at Bates's camp and you could do your thing. But with the fire danger I don't want you left alone. If you've never been in a forest fire, you can quickly become disoriented."

Libby was the first to agree. In her city of concrete, steel and glass, she had never gotten close to a major fire of any kind. "I'm glad you'll be coming along," she said. "When will we leave?"

"We'll go up tomorrow morning. Early. I've got Chuck trying to locate Bates. Apparently he wanders several miles north from his camp during the day and comes back each night. Don't worry, I'll make sure we find him. I want to be there to see his so-called condor."

Libby gawked at the beehive of activity at the main camp. When she had visited before, it had been a quiet little valley with only six mobile offices. Now another ten trailers were arranged in neat rows, attesting to the growth that had taken place.

There were gargantuan bulldozers known as Caterpillar D9s, which would shave the earth clean of all debris, making way for the road that would go far into the interior. A number of dump trucks and graders roared noisily by, kicking up yellow clouds of dust into the lazy afternoon heat. Dan picked up her luggage and guided her over to the dirt-encrusted mobile home that served as his residence.

Once inside, Libby turned to him, smiling. "This is a busy place! And you're coordinating all of it?" There was respect in her voice as she watched him take the suitcases into the bedroom. Their bedroom, she corrected herself.

"Yes. We're at peak activity now because the snow will start falling in late October," he explained, coming back out. He looked at ease in his well-worn jeans, light-blue chambray shirt and dusty boots with leather laces. Pushing a rebellious lock of hair off his forehead, he guided her to the kitchen. "Hungry?" he asked.

Libby sat down at the table. "Starved," she laughed.

Dan grinned, opening the refrigerator. "As usual." He looked at her critically. "What did you do, lose weight, Lib?"

Heat crept into her cheeks and she looked away for a moment. She had lost a good twelve pounds since returning to San Francisco. And it wasn't because of her job or the long hours she was putting in. Libby didn't try to fool herself. Being away from Dan was the cause of her loss of appetite. But he couldn't know that. He didn't want a permanent relationship, she reminded herself. His past was keeping him from making a commitment to her. A coil of sadness spiraled through her. She loved Dan without reserve, without any strings attached. She gazed up into his concerned features, a soft smile touching her lips. "I guess I missed the mountains," she said, avoiding the whole truth.

Dan went to work frying up some mouth-watering ham and potatoes. "And you didn't miss me?" he asked pointedly.

Libby fidgeted at the table, moving the salt and pepper shakers around on the surface in an effort to quell her nervousness. "Terribly," she admitted.

There was relief in his eyes as he looked over at her. "Good. Because I missed you like hell. How many slabs of ham do you want?" He held up a huge ham steak.

"Just one! They're gigantic," she protested.

Dan laughed amiably. "Remember, you're back in your mountains, Lib. High altitude and unpolluted air make for a big appetite."

She agreed. "Let me start out with one. Tonight, if I get hungry, I can fix another."

His blue eyes darkened. "I'm hungry for you," he murmured, his voice dropping in husky inference.

After spending the afternoon in Dan's office, reviewing all of Trevor Bates's reports, Libby looked at her watch. It was nearly five. She stretched languidly at Dan's desk, looking out the small window toward the stand of trees at one end of the busy valley. Getting up, she sauntered into the next room, where Dan was sitting, working intently on some documents. He looked up as she walked in.

"Done?" he asked.

"Yes."

He frowned, putting down his pen. "What do you think of Bates's reports?"

"They seem to be in order, Dan. I really can't judge without going to the base camp he's working out of." Her brown eyes glimmered. "But right now, all I want to do is take a walk in your forest. Think you can arrange that, Mr. Wagner?"

Dan responded to her lilting voice. "Better believe it," he said, standing. "Besides, I was getting tired of this paper-pushing. Come on, we'll take one of the jeeps and head across the valley. You'd better put on a long-sleeved shirt, though," he warned, coming around the desk and slipping his arm around her waist.

"Why long sleeves?"

"There's plenty of poison sumac and ivy up here at this time of year. I'll show you what it looks like, but the heavier clothing will protect your skin if you inadvertently brush against it." His hand barely grazed her cheek.

"And I for one don't want to see your beautiful skin marred by that miserable stuff."

The ride across the valley was brief. Sunlight slanted across the land, creating long shadows and shedding a golden glow on the outlying trees that stood like silent sentinels guarding the forest. Dan took her up the newly constructed timber road for five miles before pulling over and urging her out to walk among the fir and pine. A feeling of peace surrounded them as they walked hand in hand from the road into the forest itself. If Libby hadn't known there was a road to her right, she would have believed they were completely cut off from the rest of civilization.

Happily she smiled up at Dan. "How I've missed this!" she exclaimed, her voice filled with excitement. "I'd look out my office window and see canyons of skyscrapers made of steel, stone and glass, Dan." She halted, reaching out, running her fingers down the bark of a soft-needled tamarack. "I missed this," she admitted, her voice dropping to a whisper. "And this." She stroked the long needles gently. Libby turned, staring up at Dan's pensive face. "And more than anything, I've missed you, Dan. I find you the most intriguing, fascinating person I've ever met," she admitted. Catching his gaze, she added, "There's so much more I want to know about you, Dan."

He leaned down and lightly brushed her lips with a tender kiss. "I'm an open book to you, Libby. For the first time in a long time I want to share myself." He shook his head ruefully, his blue eyes glinting with humor. "Sure you didn't cast a spell on me, Druidess?"

Libby laughed. "On you? What about me? I swear,

these mountains have cast a spell on me! All I ever think about is you and your beautiful forest lands."

It was toward eight P.M. when Chuck Busch, the foreman, brought over Trevor Bates's latest report. Dan thanked him, handing the paper to Libby. They had just finished a simple but delicious meal, and Libby was lounging on the couch.

"Then it's all set?" she asked, looking up at Dan as he made himself comfortable on the couch next to her. "We're to helicopter in tomorrow morning at six A.M.?"

"Yes. If we go any later than that, Bates will be gone. I told Chuck to tell him our ETA. He'd better be there waiting for us," he growled.

Libby quickly read the hand-scribbled report. It contained counts of a number of insects indigenous to the area, and numbers of bird species as well as plants. She went back to the bird list, searching for the condor. There was nothing listed. Handing the report to Dan she said, "No condor today. I noticed in his reports for the last week that he hadn't sighted any buzzards. Could he be mistaking a buzzard for a condor?"

Dan managed a soft snort of disgust, perusing the paper. "That's my guess. Whatever it is, it was probably passing through on a migratory route, heading south for the winter." His eyes narrowed with anger as he handed the paper back to her. "I'll bet he never spots the damn thing again."

"Sometimes, Dan, field biologists tend to get slightly fanatical about a find and jump the gun. Maybe Bates is like that."

Dan shook his head, reaching over and pulling her into

his arms. "Let's forget about Bates and his phantom condor," he murmured huskily. "I don't know about you but I'm tired, and bed sounds like a good idea."

"Sounds wonderful," she agreed. Within moments Dan had hoisted her, carrying her as if she were a mere feather in his grasp. Her heart beat faster in anticipation of his wonderful skill as a lover. But it was more than that. She told herself that he couldn't make love to her the way he did and not feel something for her. But for Dan to admit he loved her would mean breaking down too many barriers from the past. Closing her eyes, Libby held him close. "Love me, Dan," she whispered.

The full moon's light sent a pale wash of silver into the small but intimate bedroom. Libby watched the lace-pattern shadow of the curtains on Dan's magnificent body as he began to undress. Her eyes widened in appreciation of his well-muscled chest and the breadth of his powerful shoulders. He dropped his shirt onto the chair, revealing the play of muscles in his back and torso. As he turned and walked toward the bed, Libby could see the unshielded hunger in his eyes. It made her breathless with anticipation as he settled down beside her. She glided her hand across his chest, reveling in his male beauty. Dan cupped her chin, raising her eyes to meet his.

"Do you know how many times a day I've dreamed of doing this?" he whispered, beginning to unbutton her blouse. His fingers deliberately grazed her breast, and a small gasp of longing escaped her lips. Libby felt her skin tighten beneath his caress. The blouse fell open, revealing the delicate lace of her bra. "Or this?" he murmured, leaning over and placing a kiss in the cleft.

Libby sighed, reaching up, sliding her arms around his shoulders. "No more than I," she whispered throatily, meeting his hungry gaze. She closed her eyes, sliding her fingers across the rugged planes of his face, feeling, sensing, imagining. The wind, the weather and the harsh rays of the sun had made his flesh strong. It was pliable beneath her exploring fingers and she lingered over each new discovery.

Dan kissed each of her fingers with delicious slowness. He gazed down at her tenderly, aware of his body tightening with explosive desire. The pale light gleamed on her golden hair, creating a halo about her head. Her brown eyes were flecked with the molten gold of passion. His gaze traveled to her lips, and he leaned down to kiss them, feeling her immediate and willing response. He tasted her depths with his tongue, slowly, purposefully building her excitement until he had her trembling with desire. He felt her shiver as his hand traveled firmly down her body from breast to hip. Without hurry he unbuttoned her jeans and finished undressing her.

She lay there before him, her skin radiant in the moonlight. The silvery glow lent an additional softness to her curves. Somehow, with the aid of the moonlight, the night was becoming a magical experience, a joining of past to present, a coupling of hearts that had always loved one another. Dan ran his hand gently around her taut breast, watching as longing grew in her beautiful eyes. He did love her, he admitted. More fiercely, more protectively, than he had ever loved any woman in his life. Libby brought those unknown emotions out in him, he thought, leaning down, tasting the budding hardness of her nipples, hearing her moan with need of him.

Tonight, he promised her silently, I'm going to love you with everything I have within me to give, Libby. I won't hold back; I want to give myself to you as you do so eagerly to me. He was thrilled, yet confused, by her ability to be so openly loving with him. Hadn't life scarred her also? How had she overcome past wounds to love so freely and unselfishly once again? He didn't know. But what he did know was that Libby, by simply being herself, was allowing him the opportunity to experience all of his emotions once again, and he loved her fiercely for that.

Libby moaned, pressing the length of her body against him, unable to fight her spiraling need of him. "Dan, Dan," she cried out softly, "please, be one with me, please. . . ." Her fingers dug deeply into his back as he positioned her beneath him. Her heart yearned for the physical contact. Closing her eyes, she arched upward, joy radiating through her as he thrust deeply into her welcoming body. She gasped. Time slowly swung to a halt as he gently brought her into rhythm with himself, obeying the commands of love.

Her breathing was shallow, her heart beating wildly in her breast as he took her beyond her wildest expectations. Throbbing fire leaped through her veins as an explosion of molten pleasure occurred deep within her. Libby fell against him, suddenly satiated and weak, needing his supporting arms to hold her. She reveled in his release seconds later, glorying in their shared joy. The silence fell kindly upon them as they rested in each other's embrace. Somewhere outside an owl hooted in the distance.

Dan raised himself up on one arm, studying her tenderly in the moonlight. He reveled in her natural beauty, the clean lines of her face, the silken texture of her long hair as it framed her features and the fragrant dampness of her skin as he rested his head against her breast. Her heart fluttered like a wild bird caged, and he gently stroked her beautifully formed hip and thigh. He had never known happiness such as this. He had never known it existed until now. Rousing himself minutes later, he traced her brow and cheek, watching her slowly open those lustrous, loving eyes.

"What are you?" he asked in wonder.

Libby stirred, delighting in his strong male body against her. "Just myself," she whispered, feeling utterly drained and deliciously filled with happiness.

Dan proffered a slight smile as he studied her. "That's a loaded statement, Druidess. You're magical, you know that? No wonder I think I'm under a spell." He caressed her cheek, holding her gaze. "Your giving of yourself is a rarity in this world, Libby," he began quietly. "And I find myself in awe of your ability to share, to give so openly. So completely."

A tremulous smile fled across her lips as she touched his jaw. "Don't you know that you're giving as much to me?" she whispered.

He stared at her for a long time, digesting her question. Finally he managed a half-smile and rolled over, bringing Libby to his side and covering them both with the sheet and blanket. "You bring out my best, Lib," he admitted huskily. And that's what I love most about you, he added silently. As he held her close, feeling the softness of her

141

breasts against his hard chest, he wanted to whisper those words aloud. He wanted to tell her he loved her, but something was holding the declaration back. Disappointed with himself, Dan eventually closed his eyes, but it was long after Libby had fallen asleep. He was holding a miracle in his arms and he lay awake for at least an hour, marveling at the joy Libby had brought him.

9

Trevor Bates's eyes narrowed as he watched the two people approaching his camp. He had a small fire going, with coffee perking in the battered, blackened pot. He stood up as they neared.

Libby broke the tense silence by offering her hand. "Mr. Bates, I'm Dr. Libby Stapleton," she greeted him. "And I believe you've already met Mr. Wagner."

Bates took her hand, giving it a shake and then quickly breaking contact. His dark-eyed gaze moved to the man who towered above both of them. "Dr. Stapleton, a pleasure. And yes, I've met Mr. Wagner. Sit down. I just got the coffee on," he invited.

Dan looked around the camp. Bates was a sloppy camper, and his negligence only increased Dan's dislike of the man. Several pieces of food wrapping lay about the campsite. There were also several cans thrown farther down the hill. Controlling his anger, Dan joined Libby at the fire.

"You know, Bates, if you want grizzly and black bear up here, keep on throwing those opened tin cans around," he growled, hunkering down.

Trevor gave him a scathing look as he poured three mugs of coffee into battered tin cups. "I don't need you playing forest ranger with me, Wagner. I happen to have plenty of experience living in the woods. The bears are too busy eating berries right now to bother with my cans."

Libby tensed, taken aback by the hatred in Bates's voice. She looked quickly at Dan, seeing the anger in his eyes. "Basically, what I'd like to do is spend a day in camp with you, Trevor," she said, pretending the volley had not been exchanged.

"Of course," Trevor muttered, watching Dan over his coffee cup. "I assume you've read all the reports I've radioed in?"

"Yes, I have."

Dan rose. "By the way, Bates, that brings up another point I wanted to discuss with you."

Bates ignored him, drinking his coffee.

"You know that thing you call a radio? I've brought you a more reliable model. It may be useful, because it has a longer range and won't conk out on you in an emergency."

"Wagner, I really appreciate your thoughtfulness, but you can keep your damn radio. My hand-held portable only weighs half a pound." He glared up at Dan. "And when I'm carrying a fifty-pound pack, I don't need a newer, better radio that weighs close to four pounds. No thanks, I'll use the one I've always had. It's never failed me yet."

Dan reined in his temper. He saw Libby give him a distraught look and thought better of verbally attacking Bates in front of her. "Have it your way," he returned, the velvet in his voice belying the anger he felt.

"I come back to camp every night," Trevor said defensively, "and I keep a larger model here as a back up. So I really don't see the problem, Wagner."

There would be one if I was going to allow Libby to stay overnight with you, Dan thought savagely. He compressed his mouth into a thin line, disliking Bates's way of camping. He remained silent, walking away from the fire so that Libby could deal with Trevor in her own way. Taking his own portable radio, which he carried around his waist on a special belt, he called into base camp to check on the morning's agenda. By eight A.M. all the trucks and various equipment would be out and working.

Libby grimaced, returning her attention to the biologist. "Trevor, I'll only be up here for a few days, but I'll be going back to base camp every night. What I'd like to do is fit into your schedule and see how everything is coming along."

Trevor, who was close to forty, with thinning brown hair, gave her a distrustful look. "Dr. Stapleton, may I inquire as to why your company sent you up here? I've worked for Cascade Amalgamated before and done a thorough job for them. My credentials are good, Doctor. Unlike some biologists"—and he looked directly at her—"I have over a decade of experience in forestry management. I just don't see the reason for your being here."

Tactfully, Libby tried to explain her presence to Bates without upsetting him. "Trevor, we're quite interested in your condor sighting. We both know that the bird is almost extinct. Naturally I want to verify the sighting so that we can protect it."

Bates slowly got to his feet, watching Wagner talking on his radio some distance away. "I don't mean to question your reasons, Dr. Stapleton, but I know Wagner, there, doesn't believe me. He and I have a personal grudge that goes back a long way." He settled his black-eyed gaze on her upturned face. "Are you sure you aren't here because Wagner doesn't believe I saw a condor?"

"No," Libby lied. "I happen to have a minor degree in ornithology, Trevor, and I hold a personal interest in your sighting." That wasn't a lie. She had majored in plants and minored in predatory birds of the world. She saw Bates's eyes widen momentarily at that bit of information. She had gone over his major and minor in college and knew that it did not include ornithology. And that meant that he could be wrong about the type of bird he'd seen.

"Libby," Dan called, coming back over.

"Yes?"

"Listen, I've got to get back to base. We've got a problem brewing with some of the union employees and Chuck can't handle it. I have to go." He stopped at her side, giving Bates a black look. "Will you be all right up here by yourself for a couple of hours?"

Bates snorted and turned away, climbing back up the rise to his tent.

Libby drew in a deep breath. "You two go at it tooth and nail, don't you?" she demanded.

Dan frowned. "Yeah, we do." He studied her clear features. "I don't want to go, but—"

"Go. I think I can accomplish more if you're not around to aggravate him, Dan. Trevor just isn't a very friendly type and he certainly won't cooperate if you're here."

He hesitated. "Damn, I hate to leave you. He's asking for trouble with bears, Lib," he said angrily. Dan gripped her arm. "Look, if bears do come, climb a tree and go just as high as you can. Don't ever try to outrun a bear, because you won't make it. Just climb a tree and stay there. I don't know how long it will take to settle this problem with the union, but I'll be back here by no later than four o'clock this afternoon. I'll give you my other radio and you carry it on you today. That way I'll have constant contact with you."

Libby grinned elfishly. "Gosh, I don't know, Mr. Wagner. All that weight. Why, I can't possibly carry a four-pound radio around with me. . . ."

"Don't start on me, too," he growled, a smile lurking in the depths of his blue eyes. "The chopper's going to be here any minute now." His fingers tightened momentarily on her arm. "I'm going to go over and find out what Bates's itinerary is today before I leave. I want to make damn sure I know where he is at all times," he breathed. "Here, take my compass. You got that Buck knife in your pack?"

Libby took the compass, noticing that the olive-green

paint had been chipped off in spots from use. She held it gently in her hands, grateful for his concern. During the last week of their trek out into the wilderness he had taught her how to use it. She had gotten so good at it, Dan had allowed her to guide them back to the base camp. She had brought them within a tenth of a mile of the actual base site.

"Yes, I have it in my pack."

"Well," he said darkly, "you carry it on your belt. You never know if you might need it. And watch out for snakes. They're all over the damn place now, soaking up the sun."

She rolled her eyes. "Don't worry, I will! That's a promise."

He gave her a pat on the rear as he turned to leave. "I'll see you later this afternoon."

Libby returned his smile, her heart filled with joy. They were working as a team once again and it felt good. And so natural. She remained at the fire as Dan talked at length with Bates. Trevor traced their route for the day on a map, which Dan marked with a felt tip pen. The chopper arrived shortly after and Libby waved good-bye, watching him take off.

Trevor scowled as she approached. "Well, I'm certainly glad to see Wagner gone. At least we can do our job without his meddling."

Libby remained silent, pulling from her pack the Buck knife, which was in a sheath, and looping it on her leather belt. Bates kicked dirt on the campfire near the edge of the small meadow. Then he looked up, searching the sky.

"Look!" he shouted excitedly. "It's the condor!"

Libby frowned, straightening up from her pack. She was standing in the deeply wooded area on the rise near the tent. She saw Bates jumping up and down, pointing skyward.

"Quick!" he called. "Come and see it!"

Libby dropped everything, jogging down the slippery pine-needled expanse. But by the time she joined Bates and put her hands up to shade her eyes from the sunrise, the bird was a mere speck in the sky.

"See?" Bates breathed excitedly. "Did you see how long his wingspan was? My God, that's phenomenal!"

She moistened her lips, turning to him. "He's too far away for me to see anything, Trevor."

Bates became excited. "I know where he's going! Let's follow him. He's going to a cliff area south of here. Yes, that's what we'll do. I'll get the camera and you get your pack, Dr. Stapleton. Hurry!"

Libby was thrown into confusion as Bates scurried around the camp like a little gnome in a furious hurry. Bates tossed her the camera, which she nearly dropped.

"Let's go! There isn't much time. He always comes this way around eight and leaves the cliffs around three to seek food. If we hurry, we can get there in time to verify that it's a condor."

"But—"

"Are you coming?" he demanded, shrugging into the pack.

Several items still needed to be put in her pack. "Well, yes, but—"

"Really, Doctor, forget all the rest of that stuff. We'll be back by nightfall," he chided as if she were some child who needed adult guidance.

She had never worked with someone who was as emotionally volatile as Bates, and it unstrung her briefly. Without a word Libby slipped on her thirty-pound pack and followed him down into the sunlit meadow.

Trevor was so intent upon making the most of their hike along the fairly flat terrain that he didn't even want to take a break. Libby insisted on one near noon, shedding her pack gratefully and sinking to the ground. Bates reluctantly stopped.

"It's just a few more miles, Doctor," he wheedled.

"It could be a mile and I'd still stop and have lunch," she replied firmly, digging into her pack for the trail mix. A thought suddenly struck her: Where was the radio that Dan had given her? There was a sinking sensation in the pit of her stomach as she quickly checked the pockets of the pack. "Oh, damn!" she exclaimed.

"What's wrong?"

"My radio. I left it back at camp."

Bates shrugged. "I've got mine right here. Don't worry."

Libby wasn't sure, remembering Dan's displeasure over the hand-held portable. "Are you sure it works?" she asked, cringing when Bates glared at her.

"Of course I am! I've had this little beauty for six years and it's never failed me. Quit worrying. Or did Wagner's know-it-all attitude rub off on you, too?"

Anger stirred in Libby and her eyes narrowed on Bates. "I don't think Mr. Wagner is entirely wrong. He's concerned for everyone's safety. The forest is very dry and the danger of fire is critical, Trevor. I don't blame him for caring what happens to us out here."

Bates scoffed. "He may care about you, but he sure

doesn't care what happens to me. He'd probably like to see me get fried out here. That way there'd be one less thing standing in the way of this lease going through."

She took a gulp of water from her canteen, trying to control her temper. "Let's get going," she muttered, realizing that if she kept Bates occupied, he'd quit complaining. She was beginning to appreciate why Dan disliked the wiry little man so much.

The going got much rougher the last few miles. And it was four P.M. before they reached the face of the cliffs on Ridge 254. Libby untied the bandana from around her forehead, wiping away the sheen of sweat from the rest of her face and neck. Worriedly she glanced at her watch again. Bates excitedly lowered his pack, taking out his binoculars.

"Trevor, I don't care what you think. I want you to call into base camp and let them know where we are," she ordered.

"Just a minute!" he answered impatiently, quickly scanning the gray and black cliffs a mile off in front of them.

Libby unscrewed the cap of her canteen, taking a good swig of water. The sun was murderously hot, the heat rising in shimmering curtains on the basalt and lava-type rock that surrounded the cliffs. They stood at the edge of the woods.

"Trevor!" Libby snapped. "I don't give a damn about that condor. Call base!"

Grudgingly, Trevor lowered his binoculars. Like a pouting child, he walked over to his pack, angrily ripping open the nylon straps and buckles. Libby stood at a distance, her face tense and worried. She had tried repeatedly to get Bates to call in and inform Dan where they were. Originally, Bates had told Dan they would be heading due north of the camp. Now, they were many miles in the opposite direction. Well, she tried to tell herself, he'll call in and Dan can send a helicopter to pick us up.

Trevor angrily jerked open the pouch that contained the radio. It flew out of reach of his hands, landing with a sharp crack on the granite a few feet away. Libby gasped.

"Don't worry!" Trevor said, going over and calmly picking it up. He twisted a knob. A frown wrinkled his forehead. He twisted another knob and then held the radio to his ear.

"Doesn't it work?" she demanded, walking up to him.

He shrugged, checking the batteries. "Something must have broken loose," he muttered.

"But we have to make radio contact or Dan will be worried sick!"

Trevor gave her a mocking glare. "Oh, come, now, Dr. Stapleton!"

She stood, confusion in the depths of her light brown eyes. If Dan did fly into the base camp at four as he'd said he would, he wouldn't find them. Libby twisted around, looking in the distance toward Ridge 256, where their base camp was located. They had spent too much time getting to the cliffs. And it would be getting dark by seven. Should she head back toward base camp at darkness, or stay where she was? Either way, Dan was going to be worried. She turned and glared at Bates.

"I hope you don't run your scientific experiments like you did this little jaunt," she said, anger in her voice. "We have a choice now. Either we stay here and hike back tomorrow morning or we start for base camp right now."

Trevor shrugged, appearing pleased. "Let's stay here, Doctor. The condor's already gone for food. Maybe, if we get lucky, he'll come back before nightfall and you can verify my findings. Don't look so worried. Wagner can sit and wait for us." He smiled, chuckling to himself as he began to gather some dry wood to start a fire later. "Maybe it'll do him some good. Well, let's make the best of this situation. Let's set up camp at the tree line. Later I'll tear the radio apart and see if I can't get it working again. I know that will make you happy."

Morosely, Libby took the binoculars at Bates's urging. It was after sunset and the dying rays of the sun were long gone from the forest. He pointed excitedly toward the deeply shadowed cliffs.

"There! Do you see him? Do you?"

Libby tucked her lower lip between her teeth, trying to site the supposed condor, which had just returned to its nesting place for the night. Finally she spotted it. "Yes— I've got it. . . ."

Excitedly, Bates hovered at her shoulder. "Well? Well?"

Libby brought the binoculars down, giving him a flat stare of disgust. "It's a turkey buzzard, Trevor. It's not a condor."

His face fell, eyes widening in disbelief. "No!" he insisted, taking the glasses from her hand and looking again. "That can't be! The wingspan on that bird is far too big for anything but a condor," he argued, his nasal voice setting her nerves on edge.

Libby was too upset and tired to argue with him. "I know a turkey buzzard when I see one, Mr. Bates. It has a fleshy red neck. Condors have fleshy necks also, but the color is more like human flesh. It's never red," she intoned, turning and going back to the camp. Maybe now he would work on the damn radio. Tiredly, Libby jerked out her sleeping bag, unzipping it and sitting on it. She unlaced her boots, slipping off her socks and putting them in the boots.

Trevor returned, grimly silent. Like a man who refused to be wrong, he dragged out a book on condors. Libby watched disinterestedly, wishing she were home with Dan at that moment.

"Will you look at the radio now?" she insisted.

Glumly, Bates put down the book, because it was too dark to read it. "Yes, I suppose I can look at it."

By ten P.M. Libby was on the verge of tears. Bates had torn the radio apart and put it together twice and it still did not work. Disgusted, he tossed the useless piece of equipment onto his pack.

"Let's go to bed. We'll get up early and make it back to base by noon tomorrow. Then you'll be happy and Wagner will be happy," he griped moodily.

Libby crawled into the sleeping bag, feeling hot and sweaty. Even at night and at that altitude, the temperature was in the low eighties. She said nothing to Bates, wishing she had never met the man. Closing her eyes, Libby willed herself to sleep, dreaming of being in Dan's protective, loving arms once again. Sometime during her tossing and turning that night, she awoke to the sound of thunder rumbling on the distant horizon, then quickly fell back to sleep.

10

Trevor gasped, spinning around, looking up at the early morning sky. "Dr. Stapleton!" he yelled.

Groggily, Libby rolled over in her sleeping bag. "What?" she mumbled, rubbing her eyes.

Bates stumbled backward, his mouth dropping open, his eyes bulging in horror. "Oh, my God! Get up! Get up!"

She jerked upright at the panic in Bates's squeaky voice. As she struggled out of the bag and to her feet, Libby turned toward him. Her eyes widened, fear stabbing through her. On the horizon, for as far as she could see, there was a dull yellow-orange glow blotting out the dawn. "What—" she gasped, running to his side, hands across her mouth. "What is it?" she gasped.

"A forest fire. A big one! God, we gotta get out of here. Fast!" he cried, nervously throwing his gear into his pack.

Anxiously, Libby looked first at the fire, which stretched horizon to horizon, and then at Bates. His movements were bordering on panic, his hands trembling. When he came to the broken radio, he threw it away in disgust.

Libby's face drew into tense lines. "No one can reach us . . ." she said, alarm eating away at her brittle calm. She turned, staring up at the orange-colored sky. Dan's words came floating back to her: If you've never been in a forest fire, you can quickly become disoriented. Forcing herself to remain calm despite Trevor's hysteria, Libby tried to think coherently.

"Trevor, get me the map. We've got to try to make our way to Camp Three. If we reach it, we can radio for help."

Shakily, Bates did as she suggested for once, without an argument. They knelt on the dry ground, huddled over the map. Libby caught the first whiff of smoke in the air and it sent her heart racing with fear. She traced the route toward the camp with her finger.

"It's here. We have to go in a south-southeast direction, Trevor." Her mind raced with possibilities. They were many miles south of their camp. Had Dan already mounted a search for them? It would be impossible to spot them from the air beneath the umbrella of forest trees.

"That camp is fifteen miles away!" Bates cried, sweat popping out on his brow. "We'll never make it! We have to go north, back to my camp. They'll rescue us there."

"No, we'll be walking right back into the arms of the fire. We can't spend half a day moving toward it, Trevor. That's suicide!"

156

The wind was picking up, coming from a northwesterly direction. Libby was sure it was pushing the fire just that much faster toward them. The sky was clear of the thunderstorms that had plagued her sleep the night before. Rain would not come to rescue them.

"We'll never make it to that camp, Dr. Stapleton!" Bates said, growing firmer, though he trembled visibly as he watched the sky growing a brighter orange. "I'm going back! I don't care what you do."

Libby gazed up at him, stunned by his decision. "You're crazy," she said stiffly, getting to her feet. "I'm going to head toward Camp Three. When I get there, I'll send word that you're working your way back to the base camp."

Bates gave her a round-eyed look of disbelief. "*I'm* crazy? You're crazier! You've got an eight-thousand-foot-high ridge and a narrow valley to cross in order to get to that camp! A person could die of a heart attack at this altitude trying to cover that kind of terrain at a fast pace!"

Libby gave him a glare. "It's better than being roasted alive by going back to your camp! Are you coming or not?"

Bates stubbornly shook his head. "No. You'll never make it. You're signing your death warrant, Doctor."

She flung him a grim smile, quickly walking over and picking up her pack. "Do me just one favor, Bates: If they do happen to get to you first, tell them my intended route so I can be rescued."

He nodded, suddenly becoming calmer. "Certainly. Good luck," he said.

She nodded, quickly packing only essential items, such as the first-aid kit, her canteen of water, a lightweight blanket and enough food to hold her for one day's worth of travel. "Good luck to you, too," she said, shrugging on the pack and nimbly tightening the straps so that it was resting comfortably on her shoulders and hips. Taking up the map and giving her compass one more check, Libby headed off in the direction of Camp Three, tossing one last look over her shoulder. Trevor Bates looked small and somehow like a gnarled old man as he slowly started up the hill toward his camp. You're a fool, she muttered to herself, turning and beginning to jog slowly down the incline.

She tried to remember everything Dan had taught her. As Libby jogged along, she tied the red bandana around her forehead. The sweat was already beginning to trickle down the side of her jaw. Fifteen miles—she didn't want to think of it as a lump sum. Setting her wristwatch, she tried to figure out how much time it would take to jog a mile. The incline would soon level out into a large meadow. She could make more time there. But would her body allow it? Libby hadn't exercised since her first hike into the wilderness. Her breath was coming in short gasps and she slowed even more to conserve her energy for the long climb ahead. Had she made the right decision? Already half of the dawn had been eaten up by the orange glow. The smell of smoke was prevalent now, the wind carrying the odor from the northwesterly direction.

It took an hour to cross the meadow and begin the climb up the steep ridge, which was dotted with huge granite formations. Sweat trickled down between her breasts, her T-shirt already soaked from her exertions, clinging to her skin. Talking to herself, Libby tried to keep calm and clear-sighted. But every time she looked over her shoulder at the orange sky, panic shot through her. The wind was changing erratically now and increasing in gustiness. She worried about Trevor. An ugly unsettled feeling stayed with her, and Libby didn't know if she was feeling danger for herself or for Bates.

Libby halted at noon, sobbing for breath. Her body was trembling, on the verge of collapse from the hard physical exertion of the climb. She stood on the crest of the ridge, the wind drying the perspiration on her glistening face. Looking north, she could clearly see yellow flames on the horizon. Her heart was pounding with fear, but she felt sadness, too: It was her forest, her trees, being destroyed by the monstrous fire. Tears trickled down her face, creating white paths through the grime and sweat. She shaded her eyes, trying to pick out the far ridge where Trevor was supposed to be. The fire seemed so close to the base camp that it sent a spasm of fear through her. Bates would die. He would die because of his own stupidity. Libby took a small sip from her canteen, grateful for Dan's warning about drinking too much water too quickly. Small sips taken frequently would be better absorbed by her dehydrating body.

She stood, resting one booted foot on a boulder, looking skyward. There, far above her, she could see what looked like World War II bombers flying toward the line of flames. Dan had mentioned that they would drop borate, a substance to smother the fire. Libby turned, realizing that she couldn't rest if she wanted to outrun the flames. Snapping the canteen back on the belt, she began her descent into the V-shaped valley below. Libby worried about Dan. He couldn't know what had happened between her and Trevor. Was he trying to find them? She knew he was. Just knowing that Dan was somehow trying to locate and rescue them gave her an incredible sense of calmness as she slipped and slid down the steep mountain on the dry bed of pine needles that covered the ground.

"Dammit, get one of those choppers back in here," Dan snapped at his foreman. "I'll go up myself!"

The base camp was a command center for the US Forest Service and firefighters who were being trucked in to halt the wildfire. Jeeps, trucks, bulldozers and hundreds of men milled around, waiting to go to the fire. Dan cursed, jerking on his hardhat and leaving the trailer to get to the radio. It was nearly one in the afternoon, and the sky was now a dull orange tinged with black. He had not slept all night, trying without success to locate Libby and Bates. At dawn he had sent a chopper to their camp, but no one had been there. Why hadn't they answered their radio? He cursed, taking long strides toward the radio tent that had been erected at the end of the string of mobile offices. He saw another large transport plane land: That meant smoke jumpers. He swallowed hard, his eyes narrowing as he ducked under the tent flap.

"Jake, raise Brent. Tell him to get back in here immediately. I want the chopper refueled and then I'm going back up with him," he ordered.

Jake nodded. "Right, boss. Brent's combing Ridge 256 one last time. They got fire reported at Bates's camp." He grimaced. "If they went back there . . ." He didn't finish, watching Wagner's face grow black with anger.

"Forget 256! It's gone," Dan snarled. "Tell Brent to fly southwest on his way in and hightail it back here—pronto!"

"Right!"

Libby! Libby! he screamed in his head. Dan walked more slowly back toward his office. His stomach churned in fear as he thought of all the nightmarish possibilities. Knowing Bates, he guessed that the idiot would lose his head. But Libby wouldn't. She had been too good a student. Had she headed toward Camp Three? It was their only hope. What if Trevor had persuaded her to take some other course of action? Dan's eyes revealed his anguish as he halted, taking the hardhat off his head and wiping away the sweat on his brow. Dammit! I love you, Libby. I can't lose you. Not like this. God, I've just found you. . . . He raised his chin, glaring in anguish up at the orange sky. Why hadn't he told her he loved her? Why hadn't he said it two nights ago, when she'd lain in his arms after they had made such wonderful, passionate love?

"Dan! Dan!" Jake yelled excitedly. "Come here! Hurry!"

Dan turned, jogging back to the tent. Jake's face was drawn with triumph. "They found Bates! Brent just radioed in. He's got a visual on him."

Dan's face became intent. "Libby? What about her? The company biologist. Is she with him?" he demanded.

Jake shrugged. "Brent said one person."

Dan went to the map. "What are the coordinates?" he snapped, his heart sinking. He had a gut instinct that Bates and Libby weren't together. Grimly he pursed his lips as Jake read off the longitude and latitude. Dan quickly traced it with his finger on the map. "Bates is south of his camp," he muttered. They had searched north of the camp for three hours the day before, trying to find them. At midnight a series of thunderstorms had ranged across the Salmon River Mountains and the forests had been turned into a roaring inferno. Dan was helpless to understand why Libby hadn't returned to Bates's camp. Had bears chased them? A cougar? Terrifying thoughts had haunted him throughout the night as he mounted a search effort to locate Libby and Bates before the approaching line of forest fire reached them. "That area is directly in front of the fire."

Jake nodded. "Brent said the chopper's heating up due to the intensity of the fire front. He was going to radio in once he picked up Bates. We should hear soon. . . ."

Dan didn't wait for the scientist to say anything when they landed. He met the chopper, ignoring the clouds of billowing dust kicked up by the rotor, jerking the door open and hauling out the disheveled Bates. He dragged the man away from the chopper. Once clear he yelled, "Where's Libby?"

Trevor cringed before Wagner. His clothes were dirty and bedraggled, torn as he had sought to outrun the fire. He sobbed, his hands and arms bloodied by his flight through thickets and heavy brush. "I don't know!" he wailed.

Dan's eyes narrowed into angry slits as he grabbed Bates's shoulders, shaking him. "What the hell do you mean, you don't know, Bates? Did you leave her?" he roared.

Bates was a rag doll in Dan's hands. "No! No! She was going to try to make it to Camp Three. I told her she was crazy! We didn't stand a chance of making fifteen miles before that fire reached us!"

Dan's eyes widened as though seeing a glimmer of hope. "Camp Three? Are you sure, Bates?"

"Yes, yes!"

Dan dragged him unceremoniously over to the radio tent, forcing Bates to stand up in front of the large map. "Show me your exact position when you left her," he ordered.

Fingers trembling, Bates took several seconds to gather his scattered thoughts. "Here—we camped here last night. We were twelve miles south of my camp. She took the map and compass. She said she would take this route," he muttered, tracing it shakily. He released Bates, letting him drop into a heap at his booted feet; then Dan turned his head, looking toward the fire. How long? How long before it reached Three? How close was Libby to the camp? There was a lake there. . . . If he could get to her, ho might be able to save her life. The fire was too close to use a chopper to try to find her. The two-thousand-degree heat fanning outward from the fire was reaching a mile in advance of the main body of flames. It could possibly destroy the helicopter, causing more loss of life. Several plans whirled in his head. Grimly he started toward the US Forest Service command post.

Libby felt her legs turning rubbery and she stopped before she fell. It was three P.M. and she could feel the ovenlike heat of the fire on her back and legs. Animals of all sizes and kinds were now running past her, trying to escape the fury of the firestorm at their heels. Her face was blackened with dirt and sweat. Her body trembled from exhaustion. She had left her pack behind, realizing that it was slowing her down. Either she was going to outrun the fire or die in the next two hours. It wouldn't matter if there was food to eat or not.

Her eyes teared from the smoke that encircled the tops of the trees. It was a deathly white fog. The heat was intense, even though the flames were still somewhere on the other side of the ridge she had climbed hours earlier. At first she had been frightened when deer, badgers and even black bears had raced by her. But they seemed to ignore the fact that she was a human being. Their panic only increased her own sense of despair. Every living thing was fleeing for its life. She panted, leaning down, trying to slow her heartbeat. After a while, she thought, I won't be able to run any longer. And the animals won't last forever, either. We'll all die.

She slowly straightened up, pain written on her features. I don't want to die! Dan! Oh, Dan, I love you, she screamed silently. Bitterly she wiped the tears from her eyes, beginning the treacherous trek down the last ridge. Somewhere on the valley floor ahead of her was Camp Three. She glimpsed a small blue lake from time to time, and the sight buoyed her sagging spirits. Libby sobbed for breath, pushed to the limits of her endurance. Just as she reached the bottom of the ridge, she stumbled. Her boot caught on a hidden tree root and she pitched forward, hands thrown outward to protect her. The earth rushed up to meet her, and then suddenly blackness closed in on her.

Libby moaned, pain stabbing through her head. Slowly she forced herself to her knees, pressing fingers against her left temple. The warm stickiness she felt was her own blood. She dazedly looked down, realizing she had landed on granite. The heat of the fire drew her attention. How long had she been unconscious? Her mouth was as dry as a cotton ball as she fought to stand. Weaving, Libby held her head, willing away the dizziness. How far did she have to go? Two miles? Maybe three at the most? The lake, a voice screamed inside her head. Get to the lake.

Semiconscious, acting out of sheer desperation, Libby began to run in the direction of the camp. Only one thought kept her from giving up: She loved Dan. They had to have the chance to make it work. She didn't want to die knowing she loved him and without being able to tell him. Drunkenly she wove between the huge, thick trees, gasping, choking on the gathering smoke.

How far had she run? Libby's legs finally gave out and she landed hard on her belly, sliding to an abrupt halt on the pine needles. Her lungs burned, feeling as if they were on fire. Her chest heaved with sobs as she lay there, unable to move an inch farther. What's more, her legs were cramping, and she had run out of water long before and was nearing dehydration. Her jeans were torn and shredded by the brush and thickets, her arms cut and bleeding. Libby buried her head in her hands, crying with frustration. It wasn't fair! She didn't want to die this way. For the first time in her life she had found a man she could love with all her heart and soul, and now the future was going to be torn away from her. Tears squeezed out of her red-rimmed eyes and she sobbed heavily, her fingers digging into the pine needles in agony.

"Libby!"

She choked on a sob.

"Libby! Can you hear me?"

She raised her head. Was her mind playing tricks on her? Had she heard Dan's voice? In her shock, had she made it up? Dazed, Libby got to her knees, unable to rise. She heard the snap and crackle of wood burning, the explosion of trees catching fire as the initial wave of heat began to sweep across the ridge. Blinking back her tears, Libby tried to see through the whitish smoke that now flowed like silent fingers of death through the trees around her.

"Libby!"

Her heart hammered in her chest. A sob escaped. "Here!" she croaked. My God, her voice was barely audible! Fighting against pain, exhaustion and dizziness, Libby forced herself to her feet, staggering in the direction of the male voice. Was it Dan? Was it? "I'm here!" she screamed, her voice cracking.

Libby suddenly halted, weaving unsteadily on her feet. There, like a dark apparition appearing out of the dense haze and smoke, was a man running toward her. She blinked unsurely, thinking she was seeing things. Her mind must have snapped. She must be imagining that it was Dan. As he closed the distance between them Libby's confusion increased. He was wearing some sort of dark-green flight suit and black boots. Why did he look like a pilot? Libby's mind began to swim and she moaned, closing her eyes. It was too much. Too much.

She felt herself falling forward in slow motion. It didn't matter anymore. She was too tired. She had run the best race she knew how and had given it her all. It hadn't been enough. Maybe now she could sleep. That was all she wanted, to sleep and forget the impending horror that was stalking her. . . .

11

~~~~~~~~~~~~~~~

Grimly, Dan checked Libby over before scooping her up into his arms. She had sustained many cuts, lacerations and bruises. Worriedly he looked at the gash on her temple. With one backward glance he gripped her tightly to him, running toward the lake, barely a mile away. It was their only hope . . . their only chance of living through the fiery holocaust. . . .

Libby felt cold water being splashed against her face. She moaned, protesting, opening her eyes. Dan's face danced before her. "Dan?" she whispered.

He nodded, cradling her next to his body, supporting her by the bank of the lake. "It's me," he rasped. His face was streaked with sweat and tense with unspoken anxiety.

"H-how did you find me?"

He smiled grimly, giving her a hug. "They found Bates

and he gave me your route over the ridge and valley. Listen," he said quickly, "we can't be rescued, Libby. The fire's too close. It's too hot. No chopper can land here right now." He spoke in a firm, soothing tone, one that was meant to keep her calm. "We've got to get in the water. The heat of the fire is over twenty-five hundred degrees Fahrenheit and we're going to get a blast of it just as soon as the flames top that ridge. No matter what happens, just trust me. I'll get us through this. But it's going to be frightening, Libby. You may panic. What ever you do, just listen to me. Just do as I tell you." His blue eyes were dark, boring into hers. "Do you understand?"

She nodded her head, looking toward the last ridge. The heat was building so rapidly that it was creating rising clouds of steam off the lake. Tears gathered in her eyes and Libby clung to him, feeling his arms go around her in a protective gesture. "Y-yes. I'll do as you say," she sobbed.

"That's my lady," he whispered, kissing her cheek. "Okay, let's get into the water."

Dan never left her side. Libby allowed him to pull her out into the knee-deep water. He led her toward a stand of thick cattails and made her lie belly-down in the water until only the tops of her shoulders and head were visible. Scooping up handfuls of mud, he swathed it over her neck and shoulders.

"We can't live underwater," he explained quickly. "So I want you to stay down on your stomach. The mud is to protect you from the heat." He reached out, putting more of the thick, gooey substance in her hands. "Smear it over your face and hair. Plenty of it, Lib," he ordered.

She had just finished covering herself with mud when

the fire crested the ridge. Dan lay down beside her, putting his arm around her. He made sure his back was to the fire, his body acting as a protection between it and Libby. The water was spring-fed and icy, soothing her hot, sweaty body. Libby pressed herself close to Dan, hearing trees explode like bombs being detonated. The air was filled with smoke and flames like ugly red welts, alive within the thunderous holocaust. She sobbed, shutting her eyes tightly. Dan's arm tightened around her waist, keeping her close.

The heat was incredibly intense. Libby felt the mud drying almost immediately and pulling at her skin. She opened her eyes only to see the sky filled with tongues of yellow, red and orange flame. Hysteria snaked through her and she began to sob. But Dan remained calm, gradually moving them into deeper water as the lake began to shrink because of evaporation. Time and again he put more mud on her head, face and shoulders. His voice, low and calming, kept Libby from struggling out of his grasp and losing total control. Time ceased. There was only the monstrous heat. Libby kept her face turned on the side, half in the water, breathing through her mouth as Dan had instructed. Her skin smarted and began to feel burned.

Dan reached down into the murky depths, pulling out a handful of lake-bed weeds. He placed it over her mouth and nose. "Breathe through this," he shouted above the roar. "Keep wetting it and breathe through it, Libby. If you don't, your lungs will get burned." She tiredly pulled the weeds to her mouth and nose, immediately grateful for the idea. Her skin stopped smarting and the air she inhaled was infinitely cooler. Everywhere she looked the world was on fire. Flames arched overhead like long, evil fingers reaching toward the horizon. Throughout, Dan's husky voice was there, comforting, his protective arm about her trembling body. And, more than anything, she kept hearing him say over and over again, "Libby, I love you. Don't give up. We'll live through this. We can do it. I love you."

She had no idea of how long it was before Dan slowly stood up in the shallow water with her leaning weakly against him. Almost miraculously the worst of the intense heat had suddenly dissipated. Libby stood dripping in the water, clinging to Dan, her eyes wide with shock as she surveyed the charred, blackened land around them. It was almost dark except for the orange glow on the far horizon to the south of them. Thousands of trees continued to burn in the wake of the blaze, flickering candles in the turbid dusk. Resting her head tiredly against his chest, she was soothed by the slow, drumlike beat of his steady heart.

Dan caressed her damp, muddied hair. "Okay?" he whispered, his mouth near her temple.

Libby nodded. "Just hold me, Dan," she managed weakly.

His blue eyes glittered in the gathering darkness. "I'll do better than that. Come on, let's wash off the mud."

She had never known that exhaustion could muddle her mind and leave her on the brink of incoherence. Dan had to bathe her like a helpless baby, repeating sentences slowly so that she could grasp what he was saying. After washing her off, Dan picked her up and took her to dry land. He gently set Libby on the ground and then unzipped a large pocket on the left leg of his flight suit. Libby watched dully, completely confused by his actions.

"What—are you doing?"

Dan pulled a long, rectangular radio out of a sealed plastic bag, turning one of the knobs to the *On* position. "Calling in our rescue." He grinned, his teeth starkly white against the blackness of his strained features. "Looks like this four-pound radio is worth carrying after all. I'm going to order a chopper in to get us out of here."

A smile pulled at Libby's mouth. She sat there in the darkness, her hair wet, looking like a bedraggled kitten. Within half an hour she heard a helicopter approaching. Dan set out a red flare, marking their position for the pilot. Once it had landed, Dan picked Libby up and carried her to the chopper. The horror of the fire lived in her and she clung mutely to Dan all the way back to base camp, finally falling into a deep, dark slumber.

Libby stirred, immediately brought awake by the protest of her stiff, abused muscles. Opening her eyes, she recognized the ceiling of Dan's bedroom. Simultaneously she realized she was in his bed. Soothing sounds entered her mind. She recognized Dvořák's *New World Symphony* playing in the background, the music drifting through the partially opened door from the living room. It was day; sunlight was filtering through the curtains. She heard footsteps and rolled onto her back, looking toward the door.

"I never thought you were going to wake up," Dan said, worry evident in his voice. He sauntered in, freshly shaven, his hair dark and damp from a recent shower.

"You realize it's almost eleven, Druidess?" he teased, sitting on the bed and placing his arm on the other side of her body so she couldn't escape.

She blinked, remembering the fire. All of it. Her brown eyes darkened with those memories as she searched Dan's rugged features. He had saved her life. Without his quick thinking, she would have died. Tears welled up in her eyes.

"Hey," Dan crooned, leaning over and brushing the tears away, "what's this?"

Libby sniffed, relishing the feel of his strong but gentle hand against her face. "It was awful!" she croaked, more tears coming.

Dan nodded gravely. "I know," he whispered, taking her into his arms. Dan held her close, rocking her gently back and forth, allowing her to cry out the fears created by the fire. He stroked her hair, marveling at its golden color, saddened that some of it would have to be cut because the fire had scorched it. She still smelled of mud and of smoke, but he didn't care; he was grateful that she was alive. The warmth of her body against him created a renewed longing, coupled with a desire always to protect Libby against anything that might cause her pain.

Dan kissed her wet cheek. "I know what will help," he murmured. "A bath. Maybe, if you get cleaned up, you'll feel a little better. And if you're real good, I'll fix you a breakfast of pancakes with dried apples and nuts in them. Is that a deal?"

Libby sniffed, having no success at banishing the tears from her eyes. Nodding, she mumbled brokenly, "Okay. I'm sorry, Dan. . . . It was all so horrible. . . . I—"

"Don't apologize, honey." He sighed heavily, releasing her. "I'm afraid that you'll have a few nasty nightmares because of the fire. It's a pretty common occurrence after you've encountered something like that."

She nodded. "What about Trevor?"

"He's alive," Dan growled. "We found him at the last minute."

"Is the fire out yet?"

"No. But they've got it under control and contained. The winds have died down and that helped a lot." He reached over, stroking her velvety cheek. "Come on, my beautiful druidess, let's get you a bath and some clean clothes."

It felt heavenly to luxuriate in the soothing perfumed water, washing away the evidence of the day before. Libby emerged refreshed and in a better frame of mind. Dan had placed his dark-blue terry-cloth robe on the hook, and she shrugged into it. It hung on her, but it was bulky and felt protective. And right then she needed that sense of security. After combing her wet hair, Libby joined Dan in the kitchen.

"Mmm," she said, sniffing the air, "it smells wonderful."

Dan looked across his shoulder, giving her an appreciative glance. "You look wonderful. Take a chair; the pancakes are about ready."

She ate ravenously, surprised at her own appetite. They lingered over coffee, their elbows touching at the table. The meal was filling.

"How do you feel?" Dan asked.

"Sore, tired and a little more stable." She gave him a searching look. "I owe you my life, Dan."

He shrugged. "Is my druidess going to go serious on me?" he teased.

Her brown eyes became shadowed as she studied his ruggedly handsome face. "Yes. I want to know what happened. How did you find me?"

Dan put the mug of coffee on the table, becoming pensive. "One of my chopper pilots spotted Bates on his way back to base. It was a lucky fluke, because we had given up the search in that area. Once they landed back here, I questioned Bates as to your whereabouts."

Libby grimaced. "We had an argument. I tried to tell him it was foolhardy to go back toward that fire. He didn't believe me."

"Well, the guy got enough first- and second-degree burns to prove he was wrong," he growled.

Libby's eyes widened. "Oh, no!"

Dan picked up her hand, turning it. "He's at a local hospital and will recover. You didn't escape without a few burns yourself. Or didn't you notice?"

Amazed, Libby saw that the backs of her hands were pink with first-degree burns. Dan gently pulled the robe back, exposing her neck and shoulders.

"Here, too. I'll put some special burn lotion on those areas in a few minutes. At least it will take the sting out of them."

"And what about you?" she demanded. "You placed yourself between me and the fire at the lake."

"I had borrowed a Nomex fire-retardant flight suit— the kind the smoke jumpers use. It kept me from getting some nasty second- and third-degree burns. I got a few first-degree burns on my neck, that's all."

Libby tilted her head, perplexed. "Flight suit?" Suddenly the image of Dan running out of the smoke toward her flashed through her mind.

"I know the head ranger who works with the Smokies. I explained the situation to him and they loaned me a suit and a parachute pack and took me up in a plane. I jumped at thirty-five hundred feet and landed about half a mile from the position I had plotted."

Her eyes widened enormously. "With all that heat, Dan? My God, you could have been killed! That wind was gusting like a tornado above the trees. . . ." Her voice became choked with tears as she stared at him. How much he must love her to risk his life in such a perilous jump.

He reached out, capturing her free hand. "It was risky," he admitted. "But everything went well. I got rid of the pack and helmet, running toward the area where I thought you would be. Before the jump I tried to estimate how long it might have taken you to make that trek under those conditions. As it turned out, I was pretty much on target." He grimaced. "A hundred other things could have happened, Libby. I didn't know if you lay exhausted somewhere up on the ridge, or if you were hurt—a broken leg . . . ankle . . ." He stopped, growing hoarse. He swallowed against a forming lump. "Libby, I loved you too much to lose you like that. It was worth any amount of risk to myself to find you."

She sniffed, fighting back the tears. "Oh, Dan, you silly, wonderful fool. You could have died, too. We were so lucky. . . ."

"I don't know if it was luck or what," he admitted quietly. "I heard you calling me right after I landed,

Libby. I heard your voice so damn clearly that I just kept following it. I'm glad you were yelling for help. Otherwise I would probably never have gone back up the slope to find you. I was going to head down closer to the lake area. I figured you would be there."

She gave him a startled look, her lips parting in amazement. "But I wasn't yelling for help, Dan. I remember collapsing from exhaustion and bawling my eyes out as I lay on the ground. I never saw you jump from the plane or anything. The first time I knew you were there was when you yelled my name."

His eyes narrowed speculatively. The silence grew between them as he ran over in his mind the events of the day before. "No . . . I *know* I heard you calling me, Libby. You called my name at least six times. I swear—"

"But I didn't, Dan."

They both stared at one another wordlessly. Libby felt her skin crawl and she shivered, suddenly stunned into introspection. Dan cradled her hand between his, caressing her fingers in the gathering quiet. He shook his head disbelievingly.

"They say that if you are protected by tree spirits, they will defend you in times of crisis. Maybe it was just my imagination yesterday, but maybe . . ."

She stood up, unable to take it all in. Hers was a world of stark reality, not myth and fable. And yet . . . She went into the living room, turning and staring back at Dan. He got up and joined her. Taking her into his arms, Dan held her tightly.

"I learned a long time ago that everything in the world isn't so easily explained," he murmured, nuzzling her hair, inhaling the fresh fragrance of her warm, pliant body. "And I know that when my smoke-jumping buddy Dave found me hanging unconscious in that tree, he swore he'd heard me yelling for help. That's how he found me. And I was out cold all the time." Dan gave a slight shake of his head. "Just thank God we're alive and together," he whispered.

Libby nuzzled against the strength of his jaw, seeking, finding his mouth. She gloried in the sensation of strength that took her breath away as he responded to her overture. His hands roved the length of her torso, coming to rest against her straining breasts, teasing them lightly. Gently, Dan pulled her to the couch and took her back into his arms.

"We still have plenty to talk about, my druidess," he murmured, stroking her hair, watching the golden highlights as the sun struck the top of her head.

Libby's breath was shallow from his fiery, branding kiss. Her heartbeat gradually slowed as she snuggled more deeply into his arms, resting her head on his shoulder.

"Believe me," she answered throatily, "I was repeating a litany of my own when I was running from that fire, Dan. I had a million things to tell you," she admitted, melting beneath his tender gaze.

"I found myself doing the same thing, Lib." He frowned, unsure of where to begin. "Up until the time I met you, I didn't want much from a woman except a good time in bed. And then you came smashing into my life." A slight smile curved his mouth. "You didn't know anything about the world I lived in; yet, you took to it like the proverbial fish to water. At first I didn't want to be saddled with you, even though I was interested in taking you to bed."

Libby gave him a scalding look and he laughed good-naturedly.

"Hey, lady, I'm being honest with you." He kissed her lightly on the cheek. "And I was right: You have a gorgeous body and the love you make is free and natural," he murmured. "That was what hooked me on you—your naturalness. Most of the women I had known played games. You didn't. In the end your honesty forced me to look at myself and what I really wanted out of life." He moved his strong fingers up her arm. "And I want you, my golden-haired druidess. I want you to be my wife and to live with me in these mountains. I know we can be happy."

Tears welled up in her wide, lustrous eyes. "I never thought—" She choked back a small sob. "I never thought you would want me for your wife, Dan."

He cocked his head to one side, a frown forming. "Why?"

She gave an embarrassed shrug, sitting up to wipe away her tears. "Oh, because you made it very plain up on that ridge after the first time we made love that you weren't about to get 'saddled,' as you put it, with any serious relationships."

He scratched his head, trying to recall the conversation. "Lib, you asked me about my past. That was how I felt *then*. But it certainly wasn't how I felt about you!" He ruffled her hair. "What am I going to do with you?" he asked gruffly, taking her into his arms and squeezing her tightly.

Libby closed her eyes, loving his ability to be so openly affectionate. "Marry me, I guess," she murmured.

"I intend to do that whether you like it or not," he chuckled. "Matter of fact, before this whole thing blew up over the condor-and-turkey-buzzard fiasco, I was planning on coming to San Francisco with this." He produced a small hand-carved redwood box. "Here, open it," he urged, placing it in her hands.

Her heart raced as she stared up at Dan and then down at the beautifully crafted box with the tiny golden latch. "Did you carve this?" she wanted to know.

"Yes," he admitted. "I had two months on my hands without the woman I loved, so I whittled a lot. 'Idle hands . . . ' Well, you know how that goes," he laughed ruefully.

Libby laughed with him, delighting in the design. Her fingers trembled imperceptibly as she sprung the latch and opened the case. The dark gleaming depths of an oval emerald ring sparkled back at her. Libby gasped, delicately touching the gorgeous gemstone. "Oh . . . Dan . . ."

He watched her closely. "Do you like it?" he asked.

Libby took the ring from the box, holding it up to the sunlight. "Like it?" she said. "I love it! It's so beautiful! Look at the different colors. . . ." She gazed up at him, adoration in her brown eyes. "I never expected . . ." she began lamely.

Dan took the ring, placing it on her left hand. The fit was perfect. "I know, you never do. That's another thing I love about you, Libby. You're one hell of a woman, but you're also a child at heart—just like I am." He held her hand, both of them looking down at the emerald. "I was never one for conventional things, Druidess. I figured I'd come to San Francisco and get down on my knees and beg you to come live with me. I was going to give you the ring even if you didn't come back with me."

"Why?" she asked slowly, touched by his admission.

"Because I wanted you to remember those wonderful three weeks here. I've always held them here," he said, pointing to his heart. "I wanted a green emerald to remind you of the forest that we both loved being a part of. Green is the color of growth, and you forced me out of my old attitudes and into a better way of looking at things." He gazed down at her, tenderness written in his blue eyes. "Green, according to the Celts, is also the color of healing. And, Libby, you healed my heart."

She reached upward, caressing his sandpapery cheek. "And you've done equally as much for me," she whispered. His mouth softly molded her lips, caressing them with reverence, with love. His eyes grew dark as he studied her with new intensity. "It's going to be my pleasure to inform Doug Adams that he's lost a biologist but gained another forester."

A smile pulled at her lips. "Do you know something? I felt like a cooped-up animal when I went back to my office, Dan. I would pace, just like you did when we first met each other. Now I understand what real freedom means." Sadness filled her tear-stained eyes. "Except now so much of our lovely forest has been destroyed."

He nodded grimly. "Just under two hundred thousand acres, Lib. It was a hell of a chunk of real estate that went up in flames. And all because of a damned lightning storm," he said sadly. He forced a smile he didn't feel. "Well, look at it this way, my beautiful druidess: We'll be planting seedlings early next spring to reforest this area."

Libby leaned against him, content as never before. "It will give me great pleasure to plant those babies," she said. "The forest gave me so much in just three weeks that if it takes a year to replant, I'll do it."

Dan smiled tenderly. "That's just like you," he murmured. "But don't worry, we'll have over a hundred men up here in late May, working in crews of twenty to do that job. It won't take as long as you think. Remember, I'm an old pro at putting back what we've taken from this land." He slid his hand across her hip. "And speaking of babies . . ." he hinted broadly.

Libby couldn't suppress a chuckle, her eyes lighting up with happiness. "Do we have to wait until next May?" she baited, a blush staining her cheeks.

Dan grinned. "No," he said seductively, gathering her up in his arms. "As a matter of fact," he continued, lifting her upward and walking toward the bedroom, "we can start on that project right now. Are you game?"

She threw her arms around his neck, laughing with him. "I should hope so, Dan Wagner!"

"Good," he said, leaning over and kissing her soundly. He placed her on the bed and then lay down beside her. "I wasn't going to wait anyway," he growled.

Her golden hair was nearly dry, tumbling across her shoulders as she rested against his body. Her brown eyes danced with mirth as she leaned her chin on his chest. "You won't get any argument from me," she declared, pressing her hips against him, delighting in his male response.

Their playful attitude suddenly changed. Dan stared down at her, realizing that, only hours before, Libby could have died. She would not be in his arms now—alive, warm, vital and loving. His blue eyes darkened and he leaned down, inhaling her wonderful female fragrance, brushing her cheek with his. "I love you," he whispered hoarsely, on the brink of tears. "I love you more than life, Libby." He embraced her tightly, forgetting how strong he was, wanting to make her a part of him forever.

Tears streaked down her cheeks as she met and matched his feverish kiss, hungrily pressing her lips to his conquering mouth. "Love me," she whispered achingly, "love me, Dan. Oh, God, I almost lost you. . . ."

"Ssshhh," he whispered against her lips. "We're alive and we're safe, beautiful druidess."

She shivered beneath his touch. It was as if they were loving one another for the first time. His callused fingers moved upward, nudging away the terry-cloth robe from her shoulders. A soft gasp escaped her lips as he brushed her straining breasts. She trembled as his mouth settled over each hardened peak, white-hot fire coursing through her body. His hand drifted lower, caressing her hips, thighs, parting her legs ever so slightly. A gasp of pleasure broke from her lips as his touch ignited a fiery hunger deep within her yearning body.

She ran her fingers across his broad chest, down his lean waist and hips, feeling him tense. The urge to show him her fierce love for him was boundless. Their bodies met in a deluge of passion amid the primal beauty of the wilderness that they both loved so fiercely. Libby arched her hips, begging him to become one with her, to celebrate their life together. Inhaling his male scent, she placed several hungry kisses on his mouth, telling him of her starving need for him alone.

Dan cupped her face, drinking in her golden gaze. He pressed a long, aching kiss upon her parted lips, telling her of his unquenchable love. He felt her quivering with desire for him as he gently entered the moist, welcoming depths of her body. He delighted in the expression of utter love in her widening eyes. This time he wanted their natural emotional outpouring to consume them until every cell in their bodies tingled with pleasure. He brought her into rhythm with himself. The thought that their love could plant the seeds of a child within her increased the sense of tenderness he felt toward Libby in those precious moments. She tensed, clinging to him, a cry of joy on her lips as she experienced the gift of their oneness. Moments later he stiffened, thrusting deeply into her, wanting to give her a child born of their love for another.

Dan lay spent, pulling Libby close to him, his arm protectively around her. She nuzzled beneath his chin, a sigh of contentment escaping her well-kissed lips. Her fingers grazed the damp carpet of hair covering his broad chest. She delighted in the strength of his musculature, a smile lingering on her features.

"If you get any better, I think I'll die of utter bliss," she whispered.

He hugged her fiercely for a long, long time. "You can

faint from bliss but not die," he corrected gently. "We came too close to losing one another."

Libby silently agreed. She rose up on one arm, gazing at his peaceful features. The love she felt for him burned fiercely within her body, within her joyous heart. She tucked her lower lip between her teeth, trying to decide how to tell him how she felt.

Dan reached out, stroking her golden hair. "What?" he inquired huskily.

She smiled with her brown eyes. "How did you know I wanted to say something?"

It was his turn to smile. "I can sense it. Or maybe I saw it in your beautiful eyes. What is it, my lovely druidess?"

She traced a pattern on his chest with her fingertip, eyes lowered, suddenly overwhelmed with emotion. "This is going to sound funny . . ." She took a deep breath, meeting his tender gaze. "I've never wanted children until now, Dan. But I want *our* children. God, how I want to feel life within me—life that we created together."

He murmured her name reverently, holding her fiercely against him. The minutes slid by in silence, both Libby and Dan content in finding peace in each other's arms.

Dan framed her face with his hands, gazing up at her adoringly. "Did you know that druids married within their own religious clans?"

Libby shook her head solomnly. "No. I thought they were celibate."

Dan laughed deeply. "Hardly, lady. A druid could only marry a druidess, and as husband and wife, they tended the sacred groves together."

"And did they have children?" Libby asked, smiling and enjoying his closeness and warmth.

"Sure did. Only they didn't call them kids."

She tilted her head, mystified. "What on earth would they call them, then?" she demanded.

Laughter lurked in the recesses of Dan's eyes. "Sprouts." And then he broke into laughter, rolling on his side and holding Libby.

She couldn't stop giggling, burying her face against his broad shoulder. "You're crazy!" she muffled.

"Mmmm, crazy in love with you, my lovely druidess," he growled, placing a kiss on her parted lips. She tasted of honey, of life itself. Dan raised himself up on one elbow, drinking in the sight of her radiant features. "And I promise you, we won't have little sprouts that will grow into trees. We'll have healthy children who will love this land as much as we do," he whispered huskily, sealing that promise with a kiss.

YOU'LL BE SWEPT AWAY WITH SILHOUETTE DESIRE

$1.75 each

1 ☐ James	5 ☐ Baker	8 ☐ Dee
2 ☐ Monet	6 ☐ Mallory	9 ☐ Simms
3 ☐ Clay	7 ☐ St. Claire	10 ☐ Smith
4 ☐ Carey		

$1.95 each

11 ☐ James	29 ☐ Michelle	47 ☐ Michelle	65 ☐ Allison
12 ☐ Palmer	30 ☐ Lind	48 ☐ Powers	66 ☐ Langtry
13 ☐ Wallace	31 ☐ James	49 ☐ James	67 ☐ James
14 ☐ Valley	32 ☐ Clay	50 ☐ Palmer	68 ☐ Browning
15 ☐ Vernon	33 ☐ Powers	51 ☐ Lind	69 ☐ Carey
16 ☐ Major	34 ☐ Milan	52 ☐ Morgan	70 ☐ Victor
17 ☐ Simms	35 ☐ Major	53 ☐ Joyce	71 ☐ Joyce
18 ☐ Ross	36 ☐ Summers	54 ☐ Fulford	72 ☐ Hart
19 ☐ James	37 ☐ James	55 ☐ James	73 ☐ St. Clair
20 ☐ Allison	38 ☐ Douglass	56 ☐ Douglass	74 ☐ Douglass
21 ☐ Baker	39 ☐ Monet	57 ☐ Michelle	75 ☐ McKenna
22 ☐ Durant	40 ☐ Mallory	58 ☐ Mallory	76 ☐ Michelle
23 ☐ Sunshine	41 ☐ St. Claire	59 ☐ Powers	77 ☐ Lowell
24 ☐ Baxter	42 ☐ Stewart	60 ☐ Dennis	78 ☐ Barber
25 ☐ James	43 ☐ Simms	61 ☐ Simms	79 ☐ Simms
26 ☐ Palmer	44 ☐ West	62 ☐ Monet	80 ☐ Palmer
27 ☐ Conrad	45 ☐ Clay	63 ☐ Dee	81 ☐ Kennedy
28 ☐ Lovan	46 ☐ Chance	64 ☐ Milan	82 ☐ Clay

YOU'LL BE SWEPT AWAY WITH SILHOUETTE DESIRE

$1.95 each

83 ☐ Chance	97 ☐ James	111 ☐ Browning	125 ☐ Caimi
84 ☐ Powers	98 ☐ Joyce	112 ☐ Nicole	126 ☐ Carey
85 ☐ James	99 ☐ Major	113 ☐ Cresswell	127 ☐ James
86 ☐ Malek	100 ☐ Howard	114 ☐ Ross	128 ☐ Michelle
87 ☐ Michelle	101 ☐ Morgan	115 ☐ James	129 ☐ Bishop
88 ☐ Trevor	102 ☐ Palmer	116 ☐ Joyce	130 ☐ Blair
89 ☐ Ross	103 ☐ James	117 ☐ Powers	131 ☐ Larson
90 ☐ Roszel	104 ☐ Chase	118 ☐ Milan	132 ☐ McCoy
91 ☐ Browning	105 ☐ Blair	119 ☐ John	133 ☐ Monet
92 ☐ Carey	106 ☐ Michelle	120 ☐ Clay	134 ☐ McKenna
93 ☐ Berk	107 ☐ Chance	121 ☐ Browning	135 ☐ Charlton
94 ☐ Robbins	108 ☐ Gladstone	122 ☐ Trent	136 ☐ Martel
95 ☐ Summers	109 ☐ Simms	123 ☐ Paige	137 ☐ Ross
96 ☐ Milan	110 ☐ Palmer	124 ☐ St. George	138 ☐ Chase

SILHOUETTE DESIRE, Department SD/6
1230 Avenue of the Americas
New York, NY 10020

Please send me the books I have checked above. I am enclosing $_____
(please add 75¢ to cover postage and handling. NYS and NYC residents please
add appropriate sales tax). Send check or money order—no cash or C.O.D.'s
please. Allow six weeks for delivery.

NAME_____

ADDRESS_____

CITY_____ STATE/ZIP_____

Silhouette Desire

Coming Next Month

Words Of Silk by Erin St. Claire

Laney McLeod had run from intimacy all her life. Suddenly, after a night with a devastating stranger during a blackout, she found herself pursued by a new responsibility and a man who couldn't forget her.

Run To Gold by Janet Joyce

Kyna had proven herself an independent woman, but she found her notions of self-sufficiency challenged when Blade jogged into her life. If love meant surrendering, why did she yearn for it?

Crystal Blue Horizon by Raye Morgan

Claire Angeli's son was lost in the mountains, and it was up to Cord McCloud to find him. Cord didn't fit into her world, but how was Claire to know that in finding her son she would lose her heart?

Buyer Beware by Marie Nicole

Casey Bennett worked to uncover mail fraud, but when her investigation cast suspicion over Simon Ashford, Casey's quest became more personal—to clear the name of the man she loved.

North Country Nights by Penny Allison

Christie had wanted a divorce from Raif—until she learned what he hadn't been willing to confide in her before. Now she was determined that pride would never again hold them apart.

Business After Hours by Laurel Evans

Nina succumbed to a stranger's charms before learning he was the literary agent she'd been warned to avoid. Abe didn't want Nina as editor to his author, but she meant to have her career *and* his love!